MURDER IN THE WINGS

A JOYCE AND GINGER MYSTERY

KATE P ADAMS

For
Karin Nieuwenhuis & Kathryn Oldfield,
with love

---

*J*oyce Brocklehurst settled herself into her seat and looked around her – perfect. The places across the aisle of the train had not been taken, and the other passengers in the first-class carriage were a small number of couples who were chatting away quietly and a smattering of businesspeople who had the misfortune of having to work on a weekend. Earphones in, they were tapping away on their laptops. This would hopefully prove to be a quiet, uneventful train ride down to London.

Joyce had insisted they get an early train, not wanting to be stuck with a bunch of tourists making their way to London for a day out, amongst them noisy and smelly kids. Joyce didn't mind children, although she preferred them barbecued to running around her train carriage on the first day of her week's holiday.

A bag and a mound of material were tossed across Joyce's eye line, followed by a body which landed heavily onto the seat opposite.

'Right, the guard helped me get your suitcase up onto the luggage rack near the door.' Ginger gave her a stern look. 'And don't think I don't know your game. There's nowt wrong with your back. I'm not going to be lifting and carrying everything for you when we get to the other end.'

'I never said there was anything *wrong* with my back; I said I had experienced a worrying twinge this morning and I didn't want to exacerbate it. It will be fine tomorrow, I have no doubt.' To emphasise her point, Joyce wiggled in her seat as though struggling to make herself comfortable.

'It's got just over two hours to be fine because you're on your own from now on.' Ginger settled herself in. She pulled out a copy of an Agatha Christie novel and a thermos flask covered in a tartan pattern from her bag.

'I hope you've got some gin in that,' said Joyce, nodding at the flask.

'Coffee,' confirmed Ginger, 'and maybe a nip of Irish whiskey. I wanted to ensure a relaxing trip down.'

'Wouldn't a nice glass of wine have been better?' Joyce whipped a can of Pinot Grigio out of her bag. It was still cold from the fridge in the shop she had bought it from and condensation had gathered on the outside. 'It's far too hot for coffee.'

Ginger was already pouring herself a drink into the lid of the flask, which doubled as a cup.

'I have the distinct feeling that my liver is going to take rather a beating on the trip so I wanted to take things easy at the beginning, and before you say anything, this does not count. If the flask had just contained whiskey, then maybe, but this is allowed.'

Joyce looked at the can longingly, and then returned it to her bag; it was far too early for wine even by her standards. She was pleased to hear that Ginger planned on enjoying herself while they were in London, though. They had a week in which to eat, drink and be merry, which meant Joyce had a week away from her role as retail manager at Charleton House, a stately home open to the public in Derbyshire where she worked very hard running all the gift shops. She was going to London largely for a different retail experience: they would shop until they dropped, or at least, Joyce would. She knew that Ginger had a list of exhibitions she wanted to see and the only retail therapy she'd indulge in would be in the crime section of various bookshops. They would meet for lunch, and then later for afternoon cocktails before a nap, dinner and more cocktails. By the end of the week, Joyce was hoping to have maxed out a couple of credit cards and significantly reduced London's stock of champagne.

The train moved off. No further passengers had joined them in their first-class carriage.

'Did you do that intentionally?' Ginger asked, running a pointing finger up and down in front of Joyce.

'What?' Joyce looked around and over her shoulder, into the carriage; she had no idea what Ginger was on about.

'*That.*' The finger became more insistent. 'Did you give the rail company a call to confirm their seat colour and make sure your outfit coordinated?' The garish red seats had yellow and blue dashes across them. Joyce was wearing a canary yellow jacket and cobalt blue wide-leg trousers. 'Even better if you'd added a little hat; you'd be perfectly attired to tell me how to fasten my seat belt and point out all the emergency exits. How long after take-off do you start serving a meal?'

Joyce took a deep breath, and then with accompanying hand movements came back with, 'You'll find the exits here, here, here and here.' With the final *here*, she added a gesture that only required the use of two fingers. When Ginger smirked, Joyce tapped her fingernails, resplendent in bright yellow polish, on the table. She could immediately see it irritated Ginger, so did it a few extra times and grinned. This week was going to be a lot of fun. Not many people could give Joyce as good as they got, so the light-hearted sparring she and Ginger took pride in was not only amusing, it also kept her on her toes.

The trip was planned as almost entirely pleasure, a much-needed holiday for both women, but the first stop they would make was more about duty than anything. After dropping their bags off at the riverside flat they would call home for the week, they would head straight back out to visit an old friend of Joyce's mother. Kenneth Gaddy had known Margaret Brocklehurst when she had been a dancer with the Tiller Girls in the 1940s and '50s and they had been very close friends. Margaret had long since died and Joyce had retained infrequent contact with Kenneth – Christmas cards, the occasional phone call when Joyce had felt guilty, or Kenneth wanted to invite her to a reunion so she could attend on behalf of her mother. She had accepted the invitations a couple of times, but the number of dancers still alive from back then was dwindling and the get-togethers were less and less frequent.

Joyce had inherited her mother's dancer's physique, her business sense and the toughness that left most other people handily terrified of her. Margaret's tough character had been hard won; Joyce's was – she would admit to herself – partly an act, but she enjoyed people's reactions and it was a useful defence mechanism.

She looked across at her travelling companion, a stout, no-nonsense woman who favoured comfort, as displayed in the loose-fitting pale-pink smock she had opted to wear for the journey. Despite the differences between the two women, the fashion-conscious Joyce knew she'd found a kindred spirit when she met Ginger Salt.

Ginger stood up. 'I'm off to find the loo, I need a Jimmy riddle.' She slid her feet back into her Birkenstocks and set off down the aisle. Joyce sighed. This was going to be a long journey.

'There's a book-binding masterclass at the British Library I have a ticket for; I want to see the Aubrey Beardsley exhibition at Tate Britain; now Dippy the Dinosaur is back at the Natural History Museum, I'd like to go and pay him a visit...' Ginger was reading from a dog-eared notebook. 'The British Museum has an interesting exhibition on at the moment. I was thinking I might head there this afternoon.'

'We're seeing Kenneth this afternoon.'

'Of course, tomorrow, then. How long is it since you've seen him?'

Joyce thought for a moment. 'Three years, give or take.'

'And what should I expect?'

'Rather dapper. His home is like an extension of one of your precious galleries, dripping with art. Adored my mother and tends to welcome me like the prodigal daughter.' Joyce hadn't said that with much enthusiasm.

'You're not as keen on him?'

'He's perfectly nice, I just didn't get close to him. He was very much my mother's friend, never became a surrogate father or some such thing. I've kept in touch more for my mother's sake than anything; he was good to her and they were each other's plus one when required. He's gay, and back in the day Mother would be his more socially acceptable date. He would be her suitor or possible father to her children when having it known that she was a single mother wouldn't be helpful.'

'Which I assume was most of the time?'

'You'd be correct in assuming that.'

'Well, I'm looking forward to meeting him. Hopefully he'll have lots of embarrassing stories to tell me about you.'

Joyce raised an eyebrow, but remained silent on the matter.

Ginger had her own reminiscing to do. She had worked in London from time to time during her career as a seamstress, helping out in the costume departments of various theatres or touring the country with productions, but she had never lived there. She only stayed for a couple of months at a time, on short contracts or when a tour schedule made it to the city, and had a real love-hate relationship with the place. She loved the theatres, the bars, the excitement and the people, but she was a country girl at heart and would eventually tire of all the bustle. Needing wide-open spaces, she was always happy to return home to Derbyshire.

This week, however, would be perfect. She could recharge her batteries with theatre and dance, art and fine food. She could get all of that in the north, of course, but there was no denying a level of excitement about the city and a week was enough for her to enjoy that, exhaust herself, and then head home to recover.

Unlike Joyce, Ginger hadn't made plans to meet up with anyone this time; she invariably ran into someone she knew when she returned to past haunts, but as time passed, she had less and less in common with many of them. There was only so much reminiscing she could do; she didn't see much point in spending hours talking about the past with people if it was because they didn't have anything new to say to one another.

But still, she enjoyed returning and fitted back into the place with ease. She loved tramping the streets of London, and had a rule that she would only use public transport if the walk to her destination was longer than forty-five minutes.

She looked across at Joyce and thought about her friend's choice of footwear. Joyce never wore anything other than vertigo-inducing high heels; something told Ginger she might not be doing a lot of walking. Joyce would be far more comfortable in a sedan chair with a couple of muscular young men running her from place to place.

Ginger thought about the incident with Nell Gwynne, the mistress of King Charles II, who when faced with a rowdy mob threw open the door to her carriage and declared, 'Pray, good people, be civil, I am the *Protestant* mistress', or a slightly more fruity word to that effect. Everything about that scene – Nell's confidence, wit, glamour, and rule breaking – screamed 'Joyce'.

'What are you grinning at?' Joyce was watching her intently. Ginger was hardly going to admit that she had been picturing Joyce as the mistress of the Merry Monarch; although, if the shoe fits…

'Oh, nothing in particular. Just the thought of a week in the city with you, my dear.'

Joyce raised a single eyebrow in apparent disbelief and Ginger went back to flicking through her notebook, resisting the urge to giggle as she continued to compare her friend to an actress who had flirted with a king while they both watched a play at a theatre, and was known for her colourful language. Ginger had once recreated a number of dresses for a stage production about Nell Gwynne, spending weeks working on many beautiful designs.

She looked up at the pile of blonde hair that Joyce had created with pins and large quantities of hairspray, and thought about her friend's vast wardrobe.

My God, Ginger said to herself, *I'm travelling to London with a one-woman theatrical production.*

3

'Joyce, come and take a look at this. I don't believe you've ever seen it before.'

The old man smiled as she joined him. There was no mistaking the child for anyone other than Joyce Brocklehurst. She recalled that she was seven years old in this photograph, wearing a silver leotard and a headdress of bright-blue feathers. The colour was pulled from her memory; the framed photograph on the wall was black and white. She was sitting on one shoulder of a handsome young man; from the ease with which he carried her, he was strong too.

Joyce turned to look at the man beside her, who was just as handsome now, even in his nineties. His skin carried heavy wrinkles, he was stooped a little, she knew that his arthritis increasingly troubled him and some days he walked with a stick; but sixty years later, she could still remember the way he would toss her up onto his shoulder in one fluid motion.

'Bloody hell, Joyce, you started young.'

'I started what young?'

Ginger had joined them and was looking at the photo, her eyes wide with fascination.

'Layering on the makeup. Use a trowel back then as well?'

Kenneth attempted to stifle a laugh and Joyce took a deep breath.

'It was entirely appropriate for the performance and you know as well as anyone the conventions of stage makeup.'

Ginger laughed. 'Just teasing, it's a lovely photo.'

One wall of the sunlit room was covered with black-and-white photos of dancers and actors, a number of posters for London theatres nestling in amongst the collections. The familiar faces of Bob Hope, Frank Sinatra and Orson Welles stared out of the pictures, side by side with Kenneth who had been a well-respected theatre director and had written a couple of successful plays. In one photograph, Noël Coward had an arm resting around Kenneth's shoulders, a cigarette held in the air. An extremely young Judi Dench beamed at the camera as Kenneth appeared to be laughing at something she had just said. Many of the photos in the display, which was a *Who's Who* of British theatre from the '40s, '50s and beyond, were signed.

The most prominently displayed pictures were those of the Tiller Girls: lines of beautiful young women, typically in mid kick or in group poses. Sequins and feathers abounded, although one photo had them in sailors' outfits with tiny shorts. There were also top hats and tails, but always lots and lots of leg.

'This is Margaret, right?' Ginger asked, pointing to a blonde-haired woman who looked a lot like Joyce.

'That is the beautiful Margaret Brocklehurst, mother of our equally beautiful Joyce. They look very alike, don't they?'

Joyce watched with pride as Ginger studied the photograph. Her mother had been beautiful at every stage of her life. She was tall with perfect posture and eyes that could pierce straight through you. The steeliness that meant she took no prisoners, which Joyce knew she had inherited, had powered her through the various challenges life had thrown her way.

Kenneth left them looking at the wall of photographs and

walked slowly to the drinks trolley, a beautiful Art Deco affair made of brass shaped to look like bamboo.

'Martini, ladies? Toast your visit to London?'

'So long as it's not dirty,' Joyce said as she leaned back to examine another photograph. She was too lazy to get her glasses out of the handbag she'd left on the other side of the room.

'Never! Delicately stirred for someone as sensitive and dainty as yourself.'

Ginger snorted. 'She's about as dainty as a porcupine.'

Kenneth laughed. 'On the one hand, I feel I should be defending the woman I think of as a family member. On the other, I admire your bravery.' His voice dropped to a whisper as he added, 'And you're not entirely wrong in your description.'

'I can hear you both. Kenneth, I expect better of you and Mother would be turning in her grave if she knew you were joining in.'

'Your mother would probably be adding a few amusing descriptions of her own. She loved you dearly, but she also knew that you had inherited her own... shall we say, strong nature?'

Joyce had a mock scowl on her face as she accepted her glass from Kenneth, and then sat on the sofa next to Ginger. She wasn't a fan of martinis, but it was a tradition with Kenneth and she'd never had the heart to tell him. Joyce crossed her long legs and sat back. Her skin-tight cream trousers pulled taut, but then she did have a tendency to wear clothes a size smaller than she really needed. She had changed into them when she and Ginger dropped their bags off; she knew better than to travel on public transport in light-coloured clothing. Heaven only knows what colour they'd have been when she got off the train. She had retained the yellow shoes and jacket, and her tight navy-blue t-shirt was cut low enough to show the world that she remained extremely pert, and with no assistance from a plastic surgeon.

Kenneth took his place on the sofa opposite. He exuded calm and grace that was reflected in the room of his large Victorian home. Everything was stylish and beautifully made; nothing was too modern. He was a man with taste and he enjoyed traditional, well-made furnishings and art that lasted throughout the generations. Cream-coloured walls displayed photographs and paintings in a way that would have made any gallery curator proud. A beautiful Persian rug marked the centre of the room, the sofas they'd sat on framing it. An antique clock ticked loudly on top of the enormous black mantel over the equally impressive fireplace. But none of it was stuffy; it was as warm and welcoming as the owner of the house.

'First of all, ladies, I must say how pleased I am to see you both. Ginger, it is a delight to meet you. I can see why Joyce feels you are an ideal travelling companion.'

'I never said that.'

'She'd never have said anything so nice, but thank you, Kenneth, I know she thinks it. Every waking minute of every single day.'

It was Joyce's turn to snort dramatically. Kenneth continued, obviously choosing to ignore their banter for a moment.

'I'm very grateful that you made the time to pop in to see me on your trip. It's always a delight when Joyce comes around, but I must confess there is a rather specific reason for my request that you visit an old man today. Joyce, do you remember Sheridan Knight?'

'Of course. We exchange Christmas cards every year, although I haven't spoken to him for a long time. Decades even.'

'Were you aware he passed away last month?'

'Heavens no. Although it's not entirely unexpected, the man was older than God.'

'True, he'd had an extremely good innings. I do wonder, though; he had started to ask a lot of questions about something that occurred many years ago, and it does cross my mind that his questions made someone very uncomfortable.'

Joyce put her glass carefully on the table in front of her.

'Are you telling me that you think a ninety-odd-year-old man who lived in a care home was murdered?'

4

*G*inger had never met Kenneth before so she had no idea if this was a particularly wild suggestion by his standards, but Joyce certainly looked surprised. She bit her tongue and let him speak.

'I don't know, that does sound rather ridiculous when I say it out loud, but he was very determined to get to the bottom of something. He'd started to ask me particular questions about a man called Scroop Harrison de Clare. Your mother knew him, Joyce, he was part of the set that some of our friends spent time with. A very wealthy and deeply unpleasant man, he was murdered in 1953 when he was thirty years old. The police were never able to identify his killer. We all joked that they would have a queue of people willing to take the blame; to be honest, we weren't entirely joking. But as he came from quite a powerful family – or at least they were back then – there was a lot of anger directed at the police.'

'Yes, I remember. Mother didn't mention him often, but who forgets a name like Scroop?'

'Was it short for something?' Ginger asked, thinking he

sounded like a character in a Dickens novel who ran a poorhouse and made a fortune off the back of other people's misery.

'No, that was his real name: Scroop Algernon Harrison de Clare.'

'What happened?' asked Ginger.

'We were all heading out to a party and had met backstage at the Palladium theatre after a show. A couple of bottles of champagne had been opened and things were quite lively. We chaps were waiting for the girls to get ready after being on stage, so we all got together gradually over the course of an hour or so.

'I recall that Scroop was being particularly obnoxious. A show he had been heavily involved in had opened to rave reviews that week, so he deserved to celebrate, but he was extremely boastful about the success being down to him. He was an investor in a number of West End productions, so was well known and courted by many who needed funding.

'At one point, Scroop disappeared and we didn't see him again. His body was found the next day, hidden behind a pile of boxes beneath a staircase. He'd been beaten to death. Theatres are full of dark corners and shadows: the perfect place to hide a body.'

There was a knock on the door and a woman poked her head round.

'Terribly sorry to disturb you, but I'm popping out, Kenneth. I forgot a few things on the list, I'll be back in about an hour.'

'Ah, ladies, this is Nancy, my housekeeper. I had her running errands for me when you arrived. Nancy, this is Joyce, daughter of Margaret Brocklehurst who I've mentioned to you, and her delightful friend Ginger.'

Nancy stepped into the room. She was a strong-featured woman with an erect posture, so it was difficult to age her, but Ginger guessed she was in her seventies at least.

'It's a pleasure to meet you both. Kenneth has mentioned your mother many times, Joyce, and I actually think I might have seen her perform. I was quite the theatregoer in my youth and I saw many revues at the London Palladium.'

Joyce and Ginger exchanged pleasantries before Nancy took her leave.

'I'm very fortunate,' Kenneth said after Nancy had closed the door behind her. 'I've known her for many years and I'm really not sure I could cope without her. It might sound like a cliché, but she really is like family. Mind you, if you sit still for too long, she'll probably start dusting you; there is such a thing as too efficient sometimes.' He smiled with a warmth that told Ginger he was only joking. 'Now, where were we?'

'Why was Sheridan interested in Scroop after all these years?' asked Ginger.

'Maybe he had too much time on his hands. I recall that he'd been rather shocked at the time; not that someone wanted to kill Scroop, but that someone we knew – someone in our social circle – had been murdered. It was rather disturbing. Sheridan loved puzzles, always had, and I think this was one for him to focus on in his final years, although it became rather an obsession. The whole thing *was* intriguing and I found myself digging around as well. Now he's gone, I feel some obligation to carry on his work. He had a couple of ideas and I think he was onto something, but I need more evidence.'

'Is there a picture of Scroop on the wall?' Ginger was keen to put a face to the name.

'No, but I dug out some of the photos and clippings I'd saved from back then.' Kenneth leaned forward and tapped the top of a shoebox that sat on the coffee table. 'This is everything I have from around the time Scroop was killed. Actually, Joyce, I thought you might like it all. I've gone through it and there's nothing that helps me, but there are a lot of photos of your mother in there. I can imagine there are quite a few you may never have seen.'

Ginger could see that Joyce's interest had been piqued. Back home, Joyce had a beautifully curated collection of photo albums and scrapbooks that covered her mother's career. She would be keen to see what Kenneth had.

'This is Scroop. It was taken the night he died.' Kenneth handed Ginger the photograph that had been resting on the lid of the box. A group of people who looked to be in their twenties and early thirties were dressed for a night out. Beautiful satin dresses adorned pretty women with bright smiles; handsome young men with slicked-back hair laughed, looking about to break into dance at any moment. Ginger guessed that a table of cocktails was just out of sight.

One of the men, whom Kenneth was pointing to, didn't look as fun as his companions. His eyes were hard and his smile was forced.

'The girl standing next to him is Audrey Valentine. Sweet young thing. For a long time, she went out with Scroop, thought he was everything she had dreamed of: handsome in his own way, charming, wealthy. He swept her off her feet.'

Kenneth stopped and examined the photograph Joyce had returned to him after she'd taken a look. Ginger probed him.

'I'm guessing things didn't end well?'

'Eventually, for Audrey they did, you'll be glad to hear, but not until she'd had a rotten time of it. Scroop went through girls like I went through martinis. But not only was he unfaithful, he was violent. I believe your mother helped Audrey cover up more than one black eye, Joyce.

'Audrey's luck turned when Maurice Ashmore, second from the right in the photo, took a shine to her and realised what was happening. Punched Scroop's lights out one evening, asked Audrey out and they were married a year or two later. He was a very nice chap and I believe she experienced the proverbial happy ending.'

Joyce had been unusually quiet during this particular conversation so Ginger nudged her with her knee.

'Alright, girl? We can hardly be boring you; I feel like we're hearing the plot for a rather dark costume drama. Maggie Smith will come waltzing in at any moment, cast as the harridan dance teacher who bangs her walking stick on the floor in time to the music.'

'I was trying to remember what Mother had said about Scroop, but nothing was coming to mind. Maybe looking through the photos will jog my memory.'

'I'd be very grateful if you did,' said Kenneth. 'Now that I've started, I'm afraid I might be developing a similar obsession to Sheridan. I've spoken to a few people and dug into a couple of archives. There were a lot of people backstage the night Scroop died and many disliked him, but the reality was he could be fun company and he paid for much of the champagne we drank. We all joked about being prepared to kill him, but I don't believe any of us would.

'He didn't interact with people he felt were beneath him if he could help it, but I doubt a stagehand would have killed him simply because he looked down on them. That's much too farfetched. As I recall, there was no one backstage that night who was out of place or unfamiliar. It was just a normal evening where we were all heading out for a night on the town. Then the police drew a blank after the murder, so it was all rather odd.'

He sighed, and then gave a little laugh. 'It's possibly just the obsession of another silly old man, but I'm deeply curious. So if you do think of anything your mother might have said, Joyce, or if those photographs trigger any memories, please let me know. I feel like I just need a couple more pieces of the jigsaw.'

Joyce agreed.

'I like a good mystery,' said Ginger, 'so I can understand your interest.'

Kenneth smiled. 'Good. Glad you don't think I'm just getting a bit dotty in my old age. Right, another round of drinks?'

Ginger was pleased that she had made Kenneth feel less silly, but if the martinis continued to flow, there might be more mysterious deaths for the police to look into. He was going to kill both his guests with alcohol poisoning.

5

*A*s they stepped out of Kenneth's house and into the June sunshine of Highgate, one of London's more expensive suburbs, Joyce sighed to herself. Ginger was pulling out her map of London. She refused to allow Joyce to use her smartphone, despite the ease and convenience. Joyce's feelings on this veered between viewing it as quaint and bloody annoying, depending on what kind of day she was having.

Kenneth lived at the end of a row of elegant Victorian houses, a stone's throw from the famous Highgate Cemetery. There, various notables tried to get eternal sleep while tourists tramped around snapping pictures, being told of their accomplishments and regaled with tales of the Highgate Vampire. Joyce felt for the long-dead residents: she liked her sleep too.

She waited for Ginger to find her bearings. Today was a 'quaint' day, helped by the fact that they were technically on holiday and as soon as they had found their seats on the train that morning, Joyce had started to relax. Eventually Ginger lifted her head from the map and, with a dramatic wave, pointed down the road.

'Thataway. We'll get the Tube. Northern line, then Jubilee,

unless you want to walk along the Thames from Waterloo? It's only fifteen minutes.'

Joyce gave her a look.

'No? Alright then. Just thought we could burn off a few calories before dinner.'

Joyce wanted to get back to the apartment they were staying in. They'd done nothing more than drop their bags off before jumping straight back into the taxi and heading to Kenneth's. She wanted to have a bath, drink a glass of sparkling wine while overlooking the Thames, and amble her way towards dinner with Ginger.

'So, what do you think?' Ginger asked. 'Do you reckon Sheridan could have been killed?'

'If Kenneth believes that, he's mad as a box of frogs, but I don't think he does. Sheridan must have been well into his nineties by now; he could have been fit enough to run marathons twice a week, but he was still likely to drop dead at any moment. It's a side effect of being old.'

'Kenneth seems pretty determined to pick up the investigation where Sheridan left off.' Ginger pulled her shopping bag further up onto her shoulder. It contained the box of photos that Kenneth had given Joyce.

'Kenneth is quite the character and he has more determination and tenacity in his little finger than we have in our whole bodies. He was very successful through hard work, not because of a wealthy or connected background.' Joyce and Kenneth hadn't always seen eye to eye on everything, but his work ethic had impressed her and she had a lot of respect for the strength of the friendship between him and her mother. He had been around a lot when she was young and he'd never treated her as a child. She liked that, having looked down her nose at most children her own age and put herself into a special category of *adult except for the age bit.*

Joyce was excited to dive into the contents of the box, but she knew she was now going to be doing it with a motive other than seeing images of her mother. Whether or not she liked it, Kenneth had put an idea in her head and she too wanted to know what had happened to Scroop. By the sound of things, he'd probably had enough enemies to give him a lifetime's supply of potential killers. Even though the police hadn't been able to work out who the culprit was at the time, she was certainly curious all these years later.

'I've always had a love-hate relationship with London,' Ginger declared, apparently apropos of nothing and disturbing Joyce's chain of thoughts. 'But on a day like today, it firmly falls into the love category.' She pointed at a wisteria that framed a pale-green door on a bright white Victorian house and was climbing towards the upper-floor windows.

'It's difficult not to love a street like this,' said Joyce, very aware of the multi-million-pound price tag that came with the properties. 'Spend a few days travelling around on the underground and you might change your mind.'

'I told you, it's love-hate. I'll find something that annoys the heck out of me by teatime.'

Joyce thought about the day's shopping she had planned for them tomorrow and chuckled to herself. Ginger would certainly hate every minute of that.

6

_G_inger looked out across the River Thames. The balcony she stood on was almost directly opposite St. Paul's Cathedral and it was one of her favourite views, if you discounted all the skyscrapers that had gone up and tried to ignore the cranes that appeared to be breeding at a rate of knots.

'Here you go, madam.' Joyce handed her a glass of chilled sparkling wine, a trickle of condensation running down the side. They clinked glasses and Joyce turned to look out at the view. 'So, who did you have to sleep with to get this place?'

'I told you, Jenny is a friend. She's in LA filming.'

'Girlfriend type friend?'

'No, just a friend type friend. I was part of a touring production of _Les Liaisons Dangereuses_; she was an actor in the company and a regular in the bar that I made my home away from home down here. We got on, became friends, and twenty years later we're still in touch. Even if she's home, I'll come and use her guest room when I'm visiting, which isn't very often these days.'

This flat fell firmly in the love London category for Ginger. It was on the top floor of a block which from the outside was a concrete 1970s monstrosity standing on the south bank of the

Thames, a stone's throw from Tate Modern, but its rather boxy gleaming white interior had been transformed into an oasis of green. Ginger flippantly guessed there were as many plants in this one flat as Kew Gardens had in its entire collection. Enormous yuccas filled corners; the bathroom was dominated by ferns and orchids, along with a particularly ugly spider plant that she knocked her head on every time she got in the bath. Shelves of cacti had become a feature of the sitting room wall. The kitchen was taken over by ivy, aloe vera and herbs, which she assumed were grown for their looks and aroma because Jenny wasn't much of a cook. There was no need for net curtains, mainly because there was no one to peer in the windows, but also because hanging plants were dotted along every sill, forming curtains of green. The furnishings were soft and low, a range of patterned rugs leading from one room to another.

It was a welcoming cocoon that it was possible to hide away in while watching the city go about its madcap business, unaware of your searching eyes. Ginger smiled as she gazed at the crowds of people pouring across the Millennium Bridge; it always amused her that no sooner had the Queen opened it and the public enjoyed a mere few hours of its use than it had been closed again for two years for being dangerously wobbly! To be fair, Ginger had experienced the wobbly bridge some years after it had reopened, but that was down to an excess of gin.

Even as the day neared five o'clock, it was still warm and Ginger was enjoying the breeze coming in off the river. She was watching a group of runners as they made their way along the Thames path below her when Joyce called her inside to look at some of the photographs. Joyce looked faintly ridiculous with her knees practically around her chin as she perched on the edge of the rather low sofa.

She seemed to read Ginger's mind. 'I find it hard to believe that Jenny is the same age as us. I'm going to need help to get up off this blasted thing.'

'Don't worry, old girl, I'll give you a tug up.'

'You better, and whatever you do, don't leave me alone in the flat. Not if I'm sat on this thing, anyway. Get down here, I want to show you some of these.'

'Why, you found another picture of you dressed up as a child version of Danny La Rue?'

'You're just jealous.'

Ginger couldn't find the words to describe how unlikely that was. She knew how to dress up, had a number of beautiful dresses she was very fond of, all of which she had made herself, and a few shoes that even Joyce would wear. She could slap on a bit of face paint and give Joyce a run for her money. But on a day-to-day basis, comfy was the name of the game, even if on some occasions the comfort level of her wardrobe caused an eye roll so large from Joyce that Ginger could hear her irises clang against the back of her head.

Joyce had scattered some of the photographs around. There were more smiling girls, lots of legs and who knows how many millions of sequins.

'Here's one of Scroop. From the date on the back, it was taken the year he was killed. It must have been before Maurice stepped in and rescued Audrey.' It was a group shot and he had his arm possessively around Audrey's waist, but he was looking across towards Margaret. Scroop didn't look too happy. 'I do recall Mother saying that Scroop made multiple passes at her and she swatted them all away. By the look of this, she was still getting his attention. There's Maurice who went on to marry Audrey.'

'Your mum was so beautiful.'

'A quality she passed down to me.' Joyce said this with a deadpan expression; there was no indication she was playing for laughs. Margaret looked as strong-minded as she did in every other photograph; she was also keeping an eye on Scroop. The dynamics of the group were leaping out from the photograph, whether it be through body language or people's gazes. This was a group with strains and stresses, and Scroop appeared oblivious to it all.

'Who's that?' Ginger asked, pointing at a photograph of six dancers with a young man standing grinning between them, looking as if he couldn't believe his luck. Cute in a boyish kind of a way, he must have been all of sixteen and probably planned on showing the photo to his mates. His long fringe was pushed tidily to one side – done seconds before the photo was taken, Ginger guessed. Trying to spruce himself up, he'd probably licked his fingers and brushed the hair away from his eyes.

Joyce turned it over. 'Jim, according to this. Lucky Jim. A fan, I'd guess, although they're backstage. Maybe he's a family member of one of the dancers or another performer. It was taken at the Palladium in 1953. I bet he spent the rest of the evening bouncing off the walls with all the uncontrollable testosterone shooting around his body. Here's another picture of Kenneth looking as suave as ever, and that, I believe, is Henry, his long-term boyfriend.'

'They make a handsome couple.'

'They do. They were also very handsome brothers, cousins or friends, depending who was around at the time. That's the '50s for you.'

'Here you all are, ready for a night out.' The picture showed Joyce looking around ten years old, her mother, and her sister Bunny, who must have been about nine.

'I remember that,' said Joyce. 'We were going to the pantomime. Kenneth had picked us up and insisted on taking some photos.'

'Your mum must have had balls to be a single parent back then.'

'Oh yes, she was a tough woman. Loving, but bloody tough. It was made easier by her parents being prepared to take us in when we were very young. I say easier, but it wasn't easy by any stretch of the imagination; her parents were furious at her for getting pregnant and didn't want a lot to do with us, but they did at least ensure that Mum didn't have to give us away. They knew that wasn't the right thing to do.

'We lived in the attic bedrooms, Mum paid rent, and as soon as we were old enough, Bunny and I had a list of jobs to do around the house as long as your arm. Mum was still touring quite a lot, even after she left the Tiller Girls, so sometimes we'd just be at home with our grandparents, which wasn't too bad. We kept our heads down. I got on quite well with Grandpa, but Grandmother… she was a miserable sod.'

'You've never talked about your father.'

'Not a lot to say, I never met him. Mum once said he was a good man, but circumstances meant they couldn't be together. I have a feeling she never actually told him she was pregnant. No one ever talked about him, and Mum got on with things. I respected her silence on the matter and didn't pursue it. I had Mum and she did the job of two parents; I never felt like I missed out.

'Bunny didn't know her dad either; he and Mum weren't married, although from the way she talked about him, I think they might have been eventually. He was killed in an accident at the factory he worked at. After that, I think Mum swore off men as bad luck. I'm sure she had some flings – she was a beauty and only human – but she never settled down with anyone.'

As Joyce spoke, Ginger considered the fact that where Margaret had given up on finding love and settling down, Joyce was on a continuing quest for romance. Three ex-husbands to date hadn't knocked her off course. Ginger had learnt more about her friend's background in the last five minutes than she had in all the time she'd known her, and she briefly wondered if Joyce was trying to find love simply because her mother hadn't.

Deciding that they'd probably done enough reminiscing for today, Ginger pulled Joyce back to the 21st century with a few well-chosen words.

'Another drink before dinner?'

'Absolutely, but you're going to have to pull me out of this chair first.'

Ginger laughed as she reached for the outstretched hand. 'Let's see if you'll need a hand remaining upright by the end of this evening.'

$\mathcal{F}$or their first evening in London, Joyce was hoping for a touch of glamour, but Ginger had insisted that she knew of the ideal place. Ginger's choice was bound to be a little... how could Joyce put it? Down to earth? Not that she minded; Ginger was fun company no matter where they went, and Joyce was more than capable of singlehandedly increasing the glamour quota, if she did say so herself. This evening, that was aided by her choice of outfit. Joyce wore a tight-fitting floral dress, which Ginger had reacted to by saying, 'That reminds me, I haven't taken my hay fever tablets today', cut low enough at the neck to display the gifts that nature had given her.

Joyce walked down the stairs into *Joe Allen's*, a restaurant not far from the Strand, feeling pleasantly surprised. She had under-estimated Ginger's taste. Ginger had said the restaurant was a favourite of the theatre scene, but experience told Joyce that a venue beloved of thespians wasn't always guaranteed to be the most salubrious of places. This was like walking directly into a very smart speakeasy: a dark space with the glow of golden lights picking out theatre posters on brick walls. Jazz played softly in the background and there was the clink of glassware and the sound of a cocktail shaker at work.

'So, what do you think?' asked Ginger as they were shown to a table.

'I think that Humphrey Bogart could walk in at any moment, and if I were to come here again, the barman would remember what drink I ordered and have it ready for me as I approached the bar,' replied Joyce as she and Ginger sat and the waiter left them to peruse the menu. 'It's that kind of place.'

'I think he'd have your cocktail and his phone number waiting for you on the bar, especially if you just happen to drop something and bend over in front of him.'

'Give over, you hardly blend into the surroundings yourself.'

Ginger's red silk t-shirt was the perfect background for her silver hair, which hung in ringlets long enough to brush the back of her neck. 'I told you to use my nail polish; I have a beautiful scarlet which would have matched that t-shirt to perfection.'

'Hmm, hooker red. Not quite my shade.'

'What are you saying, Ginger Salt?'

'Nothing, my dear. It makes you look like…'

'Go on, like…?'

'A king's mistress. Far too classy to be a hooker, you're more worthy of the role of highest-ranking courtesan in the realm.'

'That's still a prostitute.'

A very young waiter who had been waiting patiently, until now unnoticed by the two women, looked rather surprised and embarrassed as he caught the end of their conversation.

'Good evening, ladies, have you dined with us before?'

'Regularly,' said Ginger, 'although my friend here is a Joe Allen virgin.' Joyce waited for her to add to that sentence, but Ginger kept quiet. Her eyes, however, said it all and Joyce kicked her under the table.

'Can I get you a drink while you look at the menu?'

'An old-fashioned,' replied Ginger without any need for thought.

'A champagne cocktail, followed by a bottle of the Blanc de Blancs,' ordered Joyce.

'And she'd like a straw with the bottle.' Ginger grinned at the waiter who smiled back, his quivering shoulders showing that he was trying desperately not to laugh as he walked away.

'So this was your regular?' asked Joyce as she looked around.

'Of a sort. It's certainly somewhere I came at least once each time I was in town. Well, *Joe Allen's* was actually in a building up the street; this is a fairly new location for them, but it looks pretty much the same. Sadly, the ivories are no longer being tickled.' Joyce waited for her to elaborate. 'The resident pianist died about ten years ago. If he saw someone he recognised walk in, he'd start playing a tune that was a reference to a production they'd been in.'

'Talking of people being recognised, that man in the rather dated leather jacket appears to be heading our way.'

Ginger stood up so quickly you'd have been forgiven for thinking her chair was on fire, and threw her arms around the grey-haired man.

'My God, Marty, I didn't think you'd still be alive.'

'Alive and kicking, old girl, and not that much older than you. What brings you to the city? You working?'

'No, those days are largely behind me. I keep things small and local these days. We're here on a jolly.' She turned to Joyce. 'Marty Holland, meet Joyce Brocklehurst.' Joyce offered her hand and Marty kissed it.

'It's a pleasure, Joyce Brocklehurst.'

'Marty was my favourite stage manager, been in the business since he could walk. Isn't that right?'

'Before then; reckon my mum shoved me backstage in a pram and left me there.'

'Marty, join us for a drink; I have a question for you. Scroop Harrison de Clare – does the name mean anything to you?'

Marty had waved at the barman as he pulled over a chair and sat down. A waiter walked over with the drink he had left on the bar.

'Bloody hell, that's a name I haven't heard in a long time. Dead before I started doing any work in the West End, although I've heard rumours he haunts the Palladium. Why do you ask?'

'He knew my mother,' replied Joyce, deciding it was time to participate in the conversation. 'They were part of the same social circle for a while and I'm trying to find out more about him.'

'Well, I can't help you there, I'm afraid. All I know is he was wealthy, financed some shows, got himself killed, but no one was charged with his murder. Like I said, some people claim to have seen his ghost haunting the theatre, but I take that with a pinch of salt.'

'Not a believer, then?' asked Ginger as she drained her drink.

'Oh, I believe, alright; seen a couple in my time, too, but that one I'm not so sure about. Look, if you want to know more, you should talk to Jim Nevin. Works the stage door at the Palladium. He was around back then and knows all the gossip, so should be able to help. I don't have a phone number, but just pop round. I swear he never goes home so you'll find him easy enough, and I think they've got some sort of event on so he'll be working tomorrow 'n' all. Right, that's my date just walked in; I better go. Lovely to see you, Ginger. Next time you're in town we should have a proper catch-up.'

After giving Ginger another hug, he said goodbye and walked back to the bar. Joyce finished her drink and put the empty glass next to Ginger's.

'Great, so we're ghost hunting now. Where's the waiter? I need that bottle of bubbly if that's what I'm dealing with.'

'Why, you afraid of ghosts?'

'Not in the slightest.'

With impeccable timing, the waiter approached the table with the champagne, an ice bucket and a stand. Once they had a glass each, he took their order. Joyce requested the baby back ribs and Ginger a burger.

'Burger?' Joyce was confused. 'There isn't a burger on the menu.'

'Not on there, no.' Ginger tapped the side of her nose. 'It's a secret burger; you have to know to ask for it.'

'I just hope that's the biggest secret I discover on this trip.' Joyce took a large gulp of champagne. 'Make yourself useful and top up my glass.'

8

*G*inger woke to bright sunlight streaming into her bedroom. She cursed Jenny for her lack of curtains; spider plants just didn't cut it, especially after a late night with more champagne than was wise and a couple of nightcaps which had not been at all necessary. She had planned on building up her alcohol intake gradually, but the plan had fallen apart after a few glasses of bubbly. Throwing caution to the wind, she had declared, *'We're on holiday!'* before ordering a second bottle.

Joyce had told her they would be going shopping this morning, but that was only going to be possible after a bucket of very strong coffee and a large breakfast. She'd never been all that fond of shopping, but she knew that it was one of the main reasons Joyce was keen to come to London, so she was prepared to entertain her wishes... up to a point.

Ginger looked at the time: it was 9.30. She let out a groan.

'You up, girl?' There was a knock on the door and Joyce, dressed, fully made up and looking as if she'd been awake for hours, walked in with a mug in her hand. 'Come on, wakey-wakey, rise and shine.'

Ginger shuffled into a sitting position and took the mug gratefully.

'This is a pleasant surprise. Thank you.'

'Yes, well it's your turn tomorrow. I thought you could drink most grown men under the table.'

'It's the champagne, it goes straight to my head.'

'Well, you're going to have to get used to it when you're with me. Get that down you, then get yourself ready. I figure that we can do a little bit of shopping before we pop in to see Jim Nevin, the Palladium is only round the corner from Oxford Street.'

She swept out of the room, calling, 'I'll buy you breakfast,' over her shoulder. Ginger groaned again. Maybe she needed a hair of the dog. That was it: Bloody Mary was going to come to the rescue again.

The Palladium theatre was tucked down a dark and narrow backstreet not far from Oxford Circus, where some of the city's most famous shopping streets converged like the spokes on a bicycle. It wasn't uncommon for London's celebrated theatres to be found hidden away, and the Palladium wasn't one you were likely to stumble across as you wandered down a main road. It was famous not just for the big extravagant musicals that the West End was known for, but for the variety shows and musical revues which had found a home there for decades. The likes of Judy Garland, Ella Fitzgerald and Sammy Davis Jr had graced its stage. In the '50s and '60s, *Sunday Night at the London Palladium* was beamed live into homes up and down the country. It had been bombed during World War II, although the German mine didn't go off. Its cellars had been used for wine and as a wax museum. Ginger had never worked there, but she had been in the audience many times.

They walked down Great Marlborough Street, away from the

main entrance to the theatre towards a very unassuming black door with the words 'stage door' above it. Ginger loved how many stage doors were the absolute opposite to the world of glamour that they led to: not the backstage areas, which could be damp, dusty and dark, but the view of the theatre that the audience sitting in the auditorium were left with. That was a world of plush seats, gold leaf, ornate curtains; of dreams that came true; of glitz and passion. Then they made their way to the stage door to meet their idols and, at some theatres, found themselves standing outside something that resembled the entrance to a public lavatory. By those standards, the Palladium's back entrance wasn't too bad, although the building around it had been painted a rather gloomy matt black.

Walking through stage doors never lost its charm for Ginger; she always felt it was an honour and a privilege to work in the theatre, on productions that captured the audience's imagination and gave them so much pleasure, with people who she would remember fondly for the rest of her life. She got the feeling this was something Margaret Brocklehurst would have understood, and Ginger wished that she had been able to meet her. Besides which, she was intrigued by the woman who had birthed the rather remarkable and utterly unique Joyce. For that, Margaret deserved an award.

They found Jim Nevin tucked away in a tiny room just beyond the door. A counter separated him from the corridor and it was there that visitors would be welcomed and signed in, and keys collected by staff. While they waited for him to finish talking to a young man dressed in black with a radio attached to his belt, Ginger had a quick glance around his pokey office. Grey boxes with little flashing lights were attached to the wall behind him, most probably security systems or fire alarm control panels. Rows of keys hung in a lock box with its door left open. One wall was covered in photographs, much like the wall in Kenneth's home, only these pictures of performers were much more casual. They included snapshots taken at parties and pictures of Jim with celebrities. Some signed headshots included personal messages for him. Numerous cards were displayed along shelves and pinned to a cork board, all wishing *A Happy Retirement.* It looked as though the two women had caught him just in time; he probably wouldn't be here for much longer.

The man himself was medium height and medium build with grey hair. He wore a simple white shirt with a neatly tied racing-green tie. A black suit jacket hung over the back of a chair. He was so ordinary looking, you could have passed him on the street a million times and never noticed him, but now that Ginger was studying him intently, she realised she recognised him. His face held a naturally friendly smile which hid his true age, because if Ginger was right, then he really was a grand old age.

This man, she was convinced, was the boy who had appeared in the photos Kenneth had given to Joyce. He was Lucky Jim, the grinning lad who had been surrounded by half a dozen Tiller Girls and probably couldn't believe his good fortune. He must have known Margaret Brocklehurst.

'Hello, ladies, and how can I help you? Do you have an appointment to see someone?' The elderly man now turned to face Ginger and Joyce. He had a warm baritone voice, which made him perfect for a job that involved welcoming people day after day. He wasn't quite a cockney, but his accent had the distinct twang of someone who had lived all his life in London. Smart black trousers complemented his shirt and tie, and his short grey hair looked as though it had been recently cut.

'Are you Jim?'

'Jim Nevin at your service. And you are?'

'I'm Joyce Brocklehurst and this is...' Joyce paused for a moment as Jim tilted his head to one side. There was a flicker of something on his face – shock, maybe, or surprise. For a moment, Ginger thought he had stopped breathing, and then he stuttered out some words.

'Bloody hell, Brocklehurst did you say?' He stood up and came out from behind the desk to get a better view, giving Joyce a good look up and down, but not with the same leering eyes that Ginger was used to witnessing. 'Brocklehurst? It can't be, although you look just like her. You're Margaret's daughter, aren't you? Tell me that you are, you'll make an old man very happy.'

'Yes, I'm Margaret's daughter. Do you...' The final words were suffocated by the hug he gave her. As Joyce stood trapped within the man's arms, she looked at Ginger out of the corner of her eye. Joyce was not a big hugger, but the message had yet to be delivered to Jim, and Ginger was finding the whole thing very amusing.

'I can't believe it... well I never.'

He stood back, rubbing the top of his head and looking utterly flummoxed. Ginger was impressed that he remembered Margaret so clearly, and Joyce looked pleased. It was lovely that he seemed to recall her mother fondly and Ginger hoped this would make it easier for him to talk to them, maybe confide in them about a difficult time. But still, they needed him to be on the ball, his memories crystal clear, not hazy and smudged by emotion.

'Why've you come looking for me? I mean, whatever it is, I'm blown away that you're here. I just never imagined...'

'We were hoping you might be able to tell us about some people that my mother would have known when she was in London, working as a dancer. We've been told that you knew quite a few of those concerned.'

'Of course, I'm happy to help.' He looked at his watch. 'I tell you what, I get off at three o'clock today. When I've handed over, I could meet you somewhere for a drink. That would be a lot easier than trying to talk here, we'll be constantly interrupted.

How about The Clachan pub just after three? It's round the back of the Liberty store.'

'Perfect, we'll see you there.'

Joyce and Ginger, who was still smirking at the size of the hug, left a bemused-looking Jim leaning against the counter, muttering, 'Well I never.'

9

'I'm impressed,' said Ginger.

'By what?' Joyce asked as they looked for a seat in the pub.

'That you were able to control yourself, that you didn't break his arms. Hugging you like that must have been assault in your book.'

'Put it down to shock.'

'It'll be nice, though, being able to talk to someone who knew your mum back then. Hopefully he'll remember a fair bit about the crowd she hung around with; he might know something about Scroop.'

'Well, if he does know anything, I hope we can get it out of him quickly. I'm not sure I could spend too long with him fawning over me. I find it hard to imagine Mother putting up with it if he was like that when he was younger.'

'He was probably a timid little thing, in awe of all those fabulous women. His confidence must have grown over the years.'

Joyce tried to imagine any young lad being anything other than timid, surrounded by strong-willed women who had fought off huge competition to get a coveted place as a Tiller Girl, and then went on to perform incredibly strenuous routines night after night. She liked the idea of hearing more about her mother, but was determined to make sure that if either of them had to sit next to Jim, it would be Ginger.

'Two gin and tonics.' Jim placed the drinks on the table, and then settled into a chair. 'And I owe you an apology, Joyce.'

The two women waited quietly while he made himself comfortable, removing his tie and loosening the neck of his shirt before taking a drink of his pint of lager.

'I think I went a bit over the top when I saw you before. It was one hell of a surprise. I mean, I had no reason to ever think that you would walk into the theatre, and you look so like your mother. It was all a bit surreal. So I'm sorry about that.' He did look somewhat sheepish, and as much as Joyce had felt it'd all been ridiculous, she found it easy to forgive the rather sweet man in front of her. She smiled in the hope that it would put him at ease, and then decided to get him talking.

'You knew my mother well?'

'For a while, I saw her every day. It was your mother that convinced me to apply for a job at the stage door of the Duke of York's. I didn't get it – I was only sixteen – but she told me not to give up. I did all sorts of things in a couple of theatres, but eventually I got the stage door job at the Palladium and in a couple of weeks, I'll have been working there forty years. Not bad for an eighty-five-year-old.' He raised his pint as though in a toast to his achievement. 'They're throwing me a big retirement bash. Apparently, I'm something of a legend, but I find all that a bit daft. I've just been lucky enough to do something I love, so why on earth would I have wanted to move on?'

'You must have been barely into your teens when you started in theatre,' said Ginger, sounding impressed.

'You're right there. I was fifteen when I got my first job at the

Palladium. Not long after that, I met your mum, Joyce. That was quite something, I can tell you; a teenage boy surrounded by all those girls, and all those legs.' He laughed. 'At first, I didn't know where to look, but I had to get used to it. I was a call boy, you see. They didn't have any of those electronic tannoy systems so you could make an announcement and it would go through to every room. No, I had to run around the theatre, telling people when it was the half – or thirty minutes – till they were expected to be by the stage, ready for the show to start, then again at fifteen minutes. Didn't 'alf keep me fit. I went everywhere; place was like a rabbit warren, but I knew it like the back of me 'and. Mind you, it included going to all the dressing rooms where the girls were getting ready, and they weren't always fully dressed. They found my shyness quite funny and would pull me into the room and make a fuss of me. It was like having dozens of big sisters; they looked out for me. Your mum was one of the more senior dancers, Joyce, and she had a way about her that meant everyone looked up to her.'

That sounded right to Joyce. She'd always seen her mother as a strong figure – the one people would turn to if there was a problem, and she was a good choice as she never got too emotionally involved.

'They'd send me out on errands or to pass messages around the building. I got to know the girls' families, their boyfriends. They really did treat me like part of the family. It was a wonderful time. Like I said, I did go on to do other jobs: I've done set building and painting; I even did a bit of electrical work, although I wasn't very good at that. I was better at dealing with people than wires, which is why I ended up at the stage door.

'I don't think I'd have kept going if it wasn't for your mum, Joyce. I'd have given up and probably ended up working in a shop or a factory and be long retired by now, or dead. It gives me energy, you see, the theatre, which is why I'm still going strong at my age.'

He was right about the energy, he couldn't half talk. Joyce wondered briefly if that was due to nerves or excitement kicking in again, but while he was on a roll, she didn't want him to stop.

'You must have got to know my mother's friends quite well, people like Audrey Valentine, Maurice Ashmore, Scroop Harrison de Clare, Kenneth Gaddy, others from that time?'

That stopped Jim for a moment or two while he thought. Staring down at his drink as he did so, he pulled a face of deep concentration.

'I remember Scroop, of course, cos he was the one who got killed. Bloody 'orrible man, he was. I'd like to shake the hand of whoever did him in. The others – yes, I do remember them. I saw them around with your mum a lot, although she talked to me more than they did. They were friendly enough, though, very kind people. Audrey and I still send each other Christmas cards.'

Joyce found herself enjoying his company. Not because he was funny or especially charming; he hadn't told them any engaging stories, but he was warm and friendly, and most importantly, he had spent time with Margaret. He had worked with her in the theatre.

Margaret had stopped dancing when she was pregnant with Joyce, but had taken her backstage on a regular basis from when she was still a babe in arms. Sometimes it was to see her mum's old friends in their dressing rooms, but once Margaret had set up her own dance school, Joyce went to see the students perform and help manage the hordes of screaming girls as they got overexcited. She'd even seen her mum dance in full Tiller Girl costume for special events, charity fundraisers and reunions. But she hadn't seen her in her early performing days, when the theatre and dance was what she lived for; when it made her go against her parents' wishes and follow a career path that didn't appear very seemly for a young woman. That was a Margaret whom Joyce hadn't been able to witness first hand.

'It's funny, someone else has been asking questions about that time. Well, about Scroop. He's writing some sort of a book on him – family member, I think. Scroop financed a couple of productions at the Palladium and this bloke wanted to find out more. I signed him in for a couple of meetings.'

This dragged Joyce immediately out of her thoughts and she saw Ginger pull a notepad and pencil out of her handbag.

'Can you remember his name?' Ginger asked before Joyce had a chance.

'Harrison. Tobias Harrison-Hunt, a bit of a pretentious mouthful.' Jim's eyes narrowed and he looked at Joyce shrewdly. 'How come you're here now? Your mum died a while back, didn't she?'

'Funnily enough, it's Scroop who's brought us round here… sort of. We saw Kenneth Gaddy and he talked about Scroop's murder; he's been trying to find out more. It's a long story, but he's keen to try and work out who killed him, and I thought we might be able to help him out, do some of the leg work. Mind you, the excuse to learn more about my mother's time in the Tiller Girls is much more of a motivating factor.'

Jim was clearly fascinated by what she was saying.

'Well, I wish I could help. I was so young back then and largely distracted by the dancers and the stars that would turn up. I'm not sure I really viewed it as a job; it was a young lad's playground. All I remember is turning up at work the next day after Scroop vanished and the place buzzing with police, then his body coming out covered in a white sheet. It was a bit of a shock. I remember one of the stagehands gave me my first taste of whisky to help me cope with it.'

'You don't remember anything strange? Anyone backstage who wasn't normally there, or an argument? Something like that?'

He shook his head. 'It's a very long time ago, love, and we had new people backstage all the time. He wasn't a popular man, Scroop wasn't. He wasn't missed, so the gossip about who might have done it didn't go on for too long. I always put that down to people being quite grateful to whoever it was.'

Jim drained his glass. 'I'm sorry, ladies, but I have to dash.' He took Joyce's hand, his overenthusiasm returning. 'This has been a bloody treat, it really has. I loved your mum to bits and I was so sorry when she passed. But seeing you, well, it's like she's come back to visit. There wasn't anything I wouldn't have done for that woman and if there's anything you need, anything at all, you know where to find me.' He grinned at Ginger, and then left the pub.

Ginger gave Joyce a wide-eyed look. 'Do you think he breathes through his ears?'

Joyce laughed. 'Even when he's calmed down, he's a bit much. But well meaning.'

'I don't think any of that was useful, though,' said Ginger as she stirred the ice in her drink with a plastic cocktail stirrer. 'Kenneth might be on a bit of a fool's errand with this. Mind you, if he's looking for something to while away a few hours in his dotage, then this might be just the project. It'll take forever to get to the bottom of this mystery.'

'What next, then?' asked Joyce. For once, she didn't feel like heading back to the shops; if truth be told, she was getting a little tired. Last night had left her somewhat the worse for wear, too, not that she would tell Ginger that.

Ginger, of course, seemed to have guessed anyway. 'I reckon we head back to the flat and have ourselves a little nappetiser,' she said.

'What in heaven's name is a nappetiser?'

'It's a nap before dinner and it would do us both some good.'

10

---

*I*t's not that Ginger wasn't interested in clothes. After all, she'd spent many years working in the wardrobe departments of theatres or taking on private commissions to make everything from wedding dresses to waistcoats, and continued to do small jobs here and there. In fact, she loved clothes: she loved the fabric, the history and, most of all, the challenge. Ginger revelled in being surrounded by swathes of silk, cotton or velvet and seeing what she could magic up.

What she didn't get a kick out of was wandering around stuffy department stores, looking at clothes that cost a fortune when she knew she could make something just as good for a tiny portion of the price on the tag – assuming the garment had a tag at all. But that was what she found herself doing first thing on Monday morning.

They'd taken things a little easy the previous night. Their nappetiser had helped somewhat, but they only consumed one bottle of champagne with dinner and hadn't felt the need for a nightcap. Thankfully, that meant that Ginger had slept like a log, which was a good thing as she now had enough strength to restrain herself and had yet to scream with frustration or boredom, or run full tilt for the nearest bookshop. She must really like Joyce; that, or be utterly terrified of her. She concluded it was somewhere in the middle of those options.

Joyce stepped out of the changing room wearing a low-cut belted dress. The crisp white fabric was covered in black polka dots. It was very long with a slit up the side, and was, as usual, just a little too tight.

'You looking for the other 100 Dalmatians?' asked Ginger as Joyce did a twirl. Joyce put her hands on her hips and took on a 'look here' stance.

'If you're not going to take this seriously…'

'I'm sorry, I'm sorry.'

Joyce ducked back into the changing room and came out with a large-brimmed black hat and a small white handbag.

'And these – do they work?'

'Absolutely,' replied Ginger, thinking a one-word answer might be her best option. But as Joyce returned to the changing room, she couldn't control herself. 'Just promise me one thing…'

Joyce's head reappeared from around the curtain.

'If you do buy it, please don't cock your leg against any lampposts.'

Joyce disappeared out of sight and whipped the curtain across furiously. Ginger howled with laughter at her own joke while Joyce chuntered away behind the curtain.

'I'm sorry, I'm sorry, I promise I'll stop now.' She pulled a tissue out of her bag and blew her nose.

'Can I be of any help? That is a particularly beautiful dress and would be very flattering on you.'

Joyce was eyeing a garment with a pattern which resembled leaves – lots and lots of multi-coloured leaves – and the sales assistant was clearly keen for her to buy it. Ginger had noticed that this particular dress was without a tag, which meant she didn't want to know the price.

'It is rather unusual,' replied Joyce, whose voice had slipped into her faux posh pronunciation. 'I'd like to try it on, if I may?'

'Certainly, madam.'

While she waited, Ginger ran through a series of comments in her head about autumn leaves and dogs and small children throwing themselves at Joyce, or not falling over in the park or they'd never be able to find her, but decided that those opinions were better off staying in her head. Joyce was in serious shopper mode and her sense of humour had opted not to join them.

A couple of minutes later, the dress appeared with Joyce squeezed into it. Ginger was impressed. It was tight where it was meant to be tight, low where it was meant to be low, and Joyce looked particularly good in it. The assistant helped her find shoes and a bag that matched.

'That ex-husband of yours may well have been a cad, but he's made it worth your while,' said Ginger.

'I made it worth my while. Every time I pay off a credit card with his money, it's like I'm kicking him in the shins.'

'Are you sure you don't need therapy?'

'This is my therapy, Ginger, and it's working a treat.' Joyce gave a wicked little grin. Ginger had noticed that she didn't appear to be carrying any deep-seated residual anger and certainly seemed to be over the heartbreak that her ex-husbands had caused her.

'Are you going to take it?'

Joyce looked at herself in the mirror, swishing the fabric around and taking it in from all angles.

'What would the total amount be, if I included the shoes and the bag?'

The assistant did a quick mental calculation. '£890.' She smiled as though it was an absolute bargain.

Joyce looked at herself in the mirror again, and then declared, 'I'll take them all.'

Ginger gulped.

'I'll just get changed, then I'll take you for lunch, Ginger. Harvey Nichols alright for you?'

Ginger nodded, briefly wondering how much that ex-husband was worth. Then again, she didn't want to know. She was distinctly British when it came to money, which meant she didn't really like talking about it.

Joyce had been in the changing room a few minutes when Ginger started to get worried.

'Need a hand?'

'Maybe.' Joyce sounded a bit strained. 'I can't get the zip undone.'

'Come here.' Ginger bustled in uninvited. Joyce looked as if she was practising yoga, an arm bent awkwardly over her head, the other reaching up her back. 'Let me do it.' Ginger gave the zip a gentle wiggle, then a slightly more robust tug.

'Careful, don't rip the fabric.'

'I won't. Hold still.' The security tag was in an awkward position, making it hard for Ginger to get any purchase with her fingers. 'How the hell did you fasten it? That tag's in the way. Hang on, I'll... no, that's not working.'

'Is everything alright in there, ladies?' called the assistant.

'Absolutely fine,' replied Joyce, her voice once again heading for the upper end of the class spectrum.

'This isn't going to work, we need help,' Ginger decided.

'No, we have to...'

'Miss, could you give us a hand?'

The assistant stuck her head cautiously around the curtain. Joyce was starting to go red and sweat was forming on Ginger's brow.

'Oh, of course. Just let me... no... a little wiggle... oh, rats.' There was a click and a fake nail flew across the changing room.

Ten minutes later and Joyce was surrounded by three members of staff, none of whom were having any luck. Panic was starting to set in; the words coming out of the assistants' mouths were calm, but one appeared to be having difficulty breathing, another looked like she was going to cry and the third kept looking away as though that would make the problem vanish. Ginger was regretting not having a camera on her.

'We're going to have to remove the security tag, there's no other way.' Ginger had suggested that more than once and been ignored. As the staff looked at one another, Ginger realised why they hadn't acted on her suggestion a split second before one of them spoke.

'Umm, I'm terribly sorry, madam, but we can only remove the tag at the desk.'

'That's quite alright, I'll come over,' said Joyce, sounding relieved that a solution had been found.

'It's just that, the magnet we use is attached to the counter top.'

'Okay, well let's...'

Joyce paused. Ginger stood up from the armchair she had made herself comfortable in. She wasn't going to miss any of the show that was unfolding before her.

Ginger would never forget the sight of Joyce sprawled on her back along the shop cash desk, her ear pressed up against a till, wiggling back and forth until a member of staff could line up the security tag that was attached to her dress with the magnet embedded in the counter. It looked as if the assistant was wrestling a dress onto a mannequin – a mannequin that had gone extremely red and whose legs were at unusual angles as Joyce tried to shuffle into position while maintaining a small degree of modesty. Even the gallon of hairspray couldn't control her hair, which was beginning to stick out at unusual angles and straggle around her face. To give them their due, the staff all managed to keep straight faces, focusing on not tearing the expensive dress. They had even had the decency to shut the shop, but a couple of teenage girls had caught sight of what was happening through the window and were enjoying the show, snapping photos on their phones.

Eventually, mission accomplished, Joyce slid off the desk. She gave Ginger a stare that would have turned lesser mortals into stone and returned to the changing room. Five minutes later, she was back at the counter again, the dress over her arm and shoes in her hand. Her hair was immaculate and her makeup had been given a refresh.

'Now then,' Joyce beamed, 'I'll just pay, and then lunch is on me.'

Ginger had to give it to the old girl: she knew how to bounce back.

With the shop door unlocked and the staff all seeming a little shell-shocked, Joyce strode out looking as though nothing had happened. Then she leant towards Ginger and addressed her in a mutter.

'If you tell a soul, I swear I will...'

Ginger threw her hands up. 'I won't say a word.'

'You better not,' Joyce growled.

They'd taken a few steps up the street before Ginger stopped.

'You go ahead, I think I've left something in the shop. I'll catch you up.'

Joyce harrumphed and carried on, while Ginger walked back to the giggling teenagers who were still outside the shop window.

'Hello, girls, I was just wondering. The photos you took of my friend in there – any chance you could email them to me...?'

11

*I*t didn't take Ginger long to catch up with Joyce. They were a little way from Harvey Nichols when Joyce's phone started ringing. It wasn't a number she recognised.

'Hello.'

'Is that Joyce Brocklehurst?'

'I am she.' Phone calls tended to be another occasion when she adopted her faux grandeur. She liked to intimidate people into getting to the point.

'This is Nancy Binns, I'm Kenneth Gaddy's housekeeper. You were here with your friend on Saturday?'

'Yes, we were. Is everything alright?'

'No, Joyce, no it's not. It's Kenneth… he's dead. Someone broke in last night and killed him.'

Nancy burst into tears. After a couple of sobs, presumably deciding that she was so upset, she was utterly incapable of saying anything else, she hung up.

Ginger had pulled Joyce straight over the road to a café and bought them both a cup of tea; Harvey Nichols could wait.

Something a lot stronger might have been more appropriate, but they had already embarked on the drinking portion of this trip with great gusto, so she had chosen, for once, to take the sensible option. They sat outside on metal chairs that wobbled on the uneven pavement, a stream of people walking past in what seemed like one continuous wave.

'That was all she said, nothing more?' asked Ginger after Joyce had filled her in.

'That was it, she was too upset.'

'And she's really called Binns? A housekeeper called Binns?'

'I don't think that was the most significant part of the phone call.'

'Give the phone to me,' Ginger demanded. 'We need more.'

Joyce retrieved the phone from her bag and found Nancy's number, handing it to Ginger. It didn't take long for Nancy to pick up. The noise from the traffic was too loud to enable Ginger to put the call on speakerphone, so Joyce leant over the table and Ginger held the phone so they could both listen.

After a brief introduction, Ginger got stuck in. 'Nancy, I realise this is upsetting, but do you think this was a random break-in, or something else?'

'I don't know, dear, I really don't. The place was a bit of a mess: everything from the desk was on the floor and the drawers had been pulled out. A couple of the photos had been ripped from the walls, but I couldn't see anything valuable missing like his antiques. They all seemed to be okay. No doors had been forced, but then he leaves the side door to the house unlocked until he goes to bed.'

She sniffed, and then blew her nose. 'I just don't know why anyone would want to do this. He's harmless. He could be a bit snooty and was occasionally moody, but he was good to me and I know he was grateful for everything I did. He could be very generous.'

It was Joyce's turn to question the woman. 'Has he been

worried about something in particular recently? When we were with him, he was telling us about his interest in something that happened a long time ago – had it been causing him a lot of stress or upset?'

Nancy was still sniffing and Joyce hoped it wouldn't continue for too long. Sniffing drove her crazy, but she knew they wouldn't get very far if she demanded the woman *pull herself together.*

'I wouldn't say he was upset or stressed, but it was on his mind a lot. I was worried it was becoming a bit of an obsession, if I'm honest. He was very pleased you were coming; he was really hoping you might remember something about that chap he kept going on about, that Scroop, or there might be something in your mother's things. It's been all he's talked about these last few weeks.'

The cogs were starting to turn in Joyce's head. It was clear that Kenneth had become fascinated with Scroop's murder, but she had assumed that like Sheridan, he was just enjoying a puzzle to help occupy an old man with a lot of spare time on his hands. She now wondered if there was a lot more to it than that.

'Nancy, was Kenneth involved in anything else? Anything that might have got him into trouble?'

There were a few seconds of silence, and then the woman answered Joyce's question with an unusual amount of certainty.

'Not at all, no. I'd know if he was – I know everyone who comes to visit, where he goes. I can hear all his phone calls. I mean... I can... I sometimes walk in when he's on the phone and I pick up bits and pieces, accidental like.'

Joyce smiled to herself. The woman had just confessed to being a nosy housekeeper.

'Okay. One more thing, Nancy,' Ginger had softened her voice, 'and this is a really awful one, I'm sorry. Could you tell us how he'd been killed?'

There was another brief pause as Nancy blew her nose again, and then she seemed to compose herself.

'Well, I let myself in and started work, but the house was quiet. I called his name, but didn't get a response, so I thought that he was out. I cleaned the kitchen, and then did the hallway and went through to the sitting room. That was when I found him. He was sat on the sofa with his back to the door.

'When I first went in, I thought he was asleep. He often fell asleep on that sofa: sometimes he'd put his feet up and take a proper nap; sometimes he'd just doze off and wake up with a stiff neck...'

Joyce let her talk. If it made it easier for her to get the point, then so be it.

'...so I thought he must have fallen asleep and not gone to bed. Maybe that was what had happened anyway and it was how the killer found him. After I left last night, he must have drifted off. Anyway, he didn't answer when I called him from the door and I was worried cos of the mess, so I walked round and...' She started to cry again. 'They'd hit him on the side of the head. It was with one of his awards.'

Joyce and Ginger sat back in their chairs in unison, Ginger letting out a big puff of air.

'My God, Nancy, I'm so sorry you had to see that,' she said. 'And sorry we brought it all back for you.'

'You don't need to apologise, I don't think I'm ever going to forget the sight of him sitting there anyway.'

'Nancy, if we can do anything to help, you've got this phone number. Please call.'

'Thank you, dear, that's very kind of you.'

They said their goodbyes, and then Ginger looked at Joyce with an expression of worry and curiosity.

'Thoughts?'

'It could just be a break-in. It's a very nice area, so any thief can be sure to find something that'll make taking the risk worth their while. It also wouldn't take long to work out that an old man lived there on his own. A couple of days watching the house would tell them Nancy's typical arrival and departure time.'

Joyce wasn't entirely convinced by that idea, even as she said it out loud. 'On the other hand, he's been distracted, almost obsessed with the murder of a man nearly seventy years ago, and he's been determined to find out more. Someone had gone through his things, but not taken anything of value.'

'Well, I suppose that whatever happened, it won't take the police long to find out who did it. There are bound to be finger-prints or a trail of some kind.'

'Unlikely, if Nancy constantly dusts anything and everything as thoroughly as Kenneth said she does. She'd already cleaned the kitchen and hallway, and if the killer wore gloves or simply did a really good job of retracing their steps and leaving no evidence behind...'

Ginger was giving her a strange look.

'What?' asked Joyce.

'I'm trying to figure out what you're thinking.'

'I'm thinking about our chat with Jim. Maybe there was some-thing in there that could give us our first clue.'

'Clue? What do you mean, "clue"?'

'You know very well what I mean: our first clue. Our first source of information.'

'You mean you want to work out who killed Kenneth?' Ginger asked in mock surprise.

'Of course I bloody do. He was one of my mother's best friends. It's what she'd have done and if I don't, then she'll prob-ably come back and haunt me. Which, bearing in mind how cross she'd be, would not be fun.'

12

An hour later, Joyce's phone rang again. Once the short conversation had come to an end and she had hung up, she turned to Ginger.

'I guess we should have expected that.'

'Who was it?'

'The police. We were amongst the last people to see Kenneth alive and they want to talk to us. They're happy to come to us, so they'll be at the flat in an hour.'

Ginger grinned and looped an arm through Joyce's.

'Right then, we better get back and decide what you're going to wear. Wow them with your legs and we might stand a chance of learning something from them.'

'There's more to me than a mere distraction for men, Ginger Salt.'

'Yes, dear, whatever you say, dear.'

Ginger opened the door to two men in dark suits and wondered if she'd come face to face with a couple of outdated television characters. The first one, who looked as if he had bought his suit in a size too small and was struggling to keep his muscles from popping out, smiled. The older man stood a pace behind his colleague, with an air of hating everything and everyone in the world.

'Joyce Brocklehurst?' asked the friendly looking one.

'Heavens no, I buy clothes that fit.'

'I heard that,' Joyce shouted.

'Ginger Salt. Come on through.'

The smiling policeman looked a little bemused as he made his way in. Mr Misery's face remained in the same sour position. Ginger indicated that they should take a seat, having noticed that Joyce had prepared for their arrival by sitting on the futon before they entered and avoiding a public show of geriatric gymnastics as she got down, or up, from the floor-level furniture.

'Would either of you like a cup of tea?' offered Ginger. 'I'm sure Joyce would be very happy...' She saw the snarl that was creeping across Joyce's face and laughed. 'Don't worry, dear, you stay where you are. I'll put the kettle on.'

'No, thank you, Miss Salt...'

'Ms Salt,' Ginger corrected the athletic-looking officer.

'Apologies, Ms Salt. We hope we won't have to disturb you for very long. I'm Detective Sergeant Knapp, this is Detective Inspector Grey.' Ginger was surprised it was the sergeant who was taking the lead, but perhaps his older colleague was just clocking in and out until an upcoming retirement. Knapp crouched down to sit on the end of a single-seat futon with an ease that Ginger envied, while Grey appeared to decide not to risk it and reached for a dining chair.

The sergeant was looking at Joyce strangely. 'Have we met before?'

Joyce smiled at him. 'If we had, I would like to think we would have kept in touch.' She smoothed down the fabric of her skirt, and then brushed an invisible stray hair behind her ear. Ginger hoped this was an act, otherwise it was going to be painful to watch.

'Yes, I recall. We were the lead officers in a case involving the family of the Duke and Duchess of Ravensbury at their London home. Don't you work for them?'

Ginger saw the recognition cross her friend's face.

'Of course, I remember now. I believe my friends and I were able to assist you in your investigations.'

A grunt came from the corner of the room occupied by Detective Inspector Grey.

'That's one way of looking at it.' He looked at his notes. 'We believe you visited Kenneth Gaddy on Saturday, is that correct?'

It was Ginger who answered. 'We did, we were there in the afternoon. We left at about three o'clock.' Joyce nodded at Ginger's time estimation.

'And how do you know him?'

Joyce filled them in on her connection to the dead man and explained that as a visit to see him had been long overdue, their trip to the city was an ideal excuse to catch up with him. Ginger couldn't help but notice that she neglected to mention Kenneth's investigations into the death of Scroop all those years ago.

After a few standard sounding questions about whether or not they had seen anyone hanging around on the street outside, or if Kenneth had expressed any concerns about his safety or mentioned signs of previous attempts at break-ins, the two men left with a reminder from the sergeant to leave the investigating to them, insisting the women call them if they thought of anything later. Joyce remained seated, like a member of royalty whose audience with her subjects was at an end.

'What was that about?' asked Ginger as she returned from seeing the police officers out. Joyce was still sitting exactly where she'd left her, examining the card Sergeant Knapp had handed her.

'Did you spot a wedding ring?' Joyce asked.

'No, I did not, but he's too young for you by about 150 years. So, why didn't you say anything about Scroop?'

'Because there is no point making Kenneth look like a crazy old man and we have no evidence that his death is related. The police seem to think that it was motivated by theft and we should trust them. If they uncover anything else, then I will of course speak to them, but right now, we must trust our boys in blue. Or out of blue, if I have my way.' She muttered the last sentence. Ginger heard, but chose to ignore it.

'Rubbish. I know you, Joyce Brocklehurst. You have a look of... oh, I don't know. It's like a cross between curiosity and determination, as if you keep getting a whiff of something and want to follow the trail. You had it back in Buxton when that tour guide was killed at the hotel.'

'If I'm getting a whiff of something, then it must be your perfume. I shall endeavour to find something new and less toxic for you to douse yourself in each morning.'

'Give over. You're aware and I'm aware that Kenneth was sniffing around a historic murder. Are you really telling me that you want to leave it alone, despite the fear of your mother coming back to haunt you? That you don't have an ounce of curiosity about the whole thing?'

Joyce stared at her for a moment, then grinned.

'Of course not, you daft old bag. There's no way that was as simple as a break-in gone wrong. Now give me a hand. It's time we went out for dinner and decided on a plan of action.' She leaned forward with her arm outstretched and Ginger bent her knees, wanting to get her friend to her feet without doing her back in.

'You do realise this will involve sacrificing a lot of your shopping time?'

'And your museum time. But I reckon we can squeeze in a few trips here and there. I'm determined to get another handbag and

I want to add some more green shades to my wardrobe, and I can assure you that no dead body is getting in the way of that.'

13

*J*oyce had chosen the restaurant and opted for a French bistro-style venue just off Covent Garden. She wanted a quiet – by Joyce's standards – dinner where she and Ginger could consider their options and plan their next move without being interrupted. It was a lively restaurant with lots of aged mirrors and servers in red waistcoats, bustling without being too loud or crowded.

After Joyce had placed her order for duck breast and Ginger moules marinière and frites, Joyce pulled out a notepad.

'While you took a bath, I went through some of the photos in the box Kenneth gave me and I managed to pull out some names that might be interesting. I wanted to know more about the people in that photograph of them all looking like they were on a night out, which we know was taken around the time Scroop was killed. Scroop used to knock Audrey Valentine about and she went on to marry Maurice Ashmore. I looked up the family online and, although Maurice died two years ago, Audrey is living in an area called Walton-on-Thames. I'm sure I can track down her exact address from another of my mother's old dancing contacts. It's not very far and we can get a train there in order to talk to her. It would be good to know if Kenneth or Sheridan made contact in recent months. I would guess that she'll be delighted to see the daughter of her old friend Margaret.'

Joyce paused to smile at the server who had brought their drinks over. He placed an Aviation in front of Joyce and a Manhattan in front of Ginger.

'If you don't mind me asking,' he said tentatively. 'I was talking to some of my colleagues and we were wondering... are you famous?'

The two women looked up at the young server and paused before glancing swiftly at one another. Joyce knew his game.

'We are extremely famous. My friend here is a very well-known dress designer who has many celebrity clients and I am a dancer and model. My face has been on billboards and in magazines all over the world.'

'I thought so.' He smiled and walked away.

'And on cards in phone boxes. What was that about?' Ginger asked.

'Young Mr Smooth there is hoping for a particularly large tip in return for some ego flattering. Anyway, we should go and see Audrey. Next on my list is Nancy, Kenneth's housekeeper. She knows plenty, I'm sure, and if there was something going on and the death is more suspicious than a break-in gone wrong, she's going to know about that too. Detectives Nice and Grumpy didn't give any indication that they were looking at it being more than a robbery, which tells me that Nancy kept as quiet about the Scroop investigation as we did.'

'That's if there is anything worthwhile for her to keep quiet about.'

'And that is what we will find out tomorrow morning when we are having coffee with her.' Joyce gave a nod of finality.

'Oh, we are, are we?'

'Yes, that was something else I did while you took a bath. I was starting to wonder if you'd moved in.'

'Baths are my quiet time, my therapy, and I need some very intense therapy when I travel with you.'

'You didn't have to come.'

'You'd have been bereft if I hadn't.'

Joyce gave a laugh of derision, but silently acknowledged to herself that she probably would have been a little upset if Ginger hadn't joined her.

'Did you dig up any more information while I recharged my batteries after another exhausting day in your company?'

'I did, I had plenty of time. Jim mentioned a relative of Scroop, Tobias Harrison-Hunt. He was an investment banker and is now a full time author – a couple of history books, a biography of Dowager someone or other from his mother's side. He's involved in a variety of charitable organisations and the family name has been given to a couple of foundations, including the Scroop Harrison de Clare Foundation for Arts and Heritage, along with a number of scholarships to dance schools under Scroop's name.'

'And we know for sure Tobias is researching Scroop?'

Joyce shook her head. 'We only have Jim's word to go on, but it's something we need to check out.'

Ginger stuck a finger in her drink and pulled out a cherry. She chewed on it and looked as if she was in deep thought.

'What?' demanded Joyce.

'We might have to be careful how we approach Harrison. We'd be asking about a member of his family, and one who wasn't a particularly pleasant person by all accounts. He might be quite defensive, and who knows? He might have inherited his ancestor's violent streak. How are they related anyway?'

'He's Scroop's great-nephew and we'll think of something. He's bound to be doing a book signing or a talk that we can get tickets for.' Joyce looked up from her notes.

'I'm rather looking forward to this.' Ginger grinned back and picked up her glass.

'Agreed. Here's to a rather more interesting trip to the ol' Smoke than we had intended.'

They were on the dessert course when Ginger asked Joyce a question she hadn't considered until now.

'Do you think this is what Kenneth intended when he spoke to us?'

'That we'd be investigating his murder? Unless he was psychic, I doubt it.'

'No, I mean that we would dive in and start investigating Scroop's murder for him. He was getting on a bit and maybe he wanted us to take over.'

Joyce thought for a moment. 'Perhaps, but he didn't actually ask.'

'Not outright, no, but maybe he thought you'd get curious or find something in that box. Maybe it was subconscious and this *is* what he wanted, he just didn't know it himself. He'd be very grateful if he knew what we're doing, what you're doing.'

They disappeared into their own thoughts and continued eating the rich chocolate mousse they had both ordered. Joyce wondered if it really had been Kenneth's intention. It wasn't like him to be shy, so she was surprised he hadn't asked outright if it was what she wanted. Either way, it was what she was doing. She hadn't kept in touch with him as much as she ought, as much as her mother would have wanted her to, and she felt a little pang of guilt. She should have paid him more attention in life, not death, so if there was something more suspicious behind his death than a robbery, she owed it to him to find out. Her mother would have wanted it too.

Joyce looked up to see Ginger staring at her.

'She'd be very grateful. Proud 'n' all, your mum.'

'What are you, blooming psychic?'

Ginger smiled. 'Well, she would. Very proud.'

Joyce wasn't too keen on being the centre of mushy attention. Other kinds of attention were fine, but not this sort.

'She always was. I was a remarkable daughter, better than she could have ever hoped for. Perfect, in fact.'

Ginger rolled her eyes and went back to her dessert. Good. Soppy moment averted.

14

*J*oyce had arranged to meet Nancy for coffee first thing in the morning. After that, she wanted to fit in some shopping and Ginger was determined to see an exhibition about Egyptian hieroglyphs at the British Museum before they continued with their quest to find Kenneth's killer.

An early start to the day had been helped by the sun streaming into the flat and a beautiful view across the Thames, both of which gave them an extra boost of energy. Joyce had agreed they would meet Nancy in a café not all that far from Kenneth's home on the edge of Hampstead Heath, a large open grassland that would be popular on a day as beautiful as today. Ginger rather fancied a hike or a dip in one of the bathing ponds while they were there, but she had reluctantly accepted that the day's tight schedule made it impossible.

They made themselves comfortable at an outside table. It was early enough that the birds weren't yet circling for the crumbs that would appear as the café got busier and plates of pastries and sandwiches became the target for sharp beaks.

Ginger was concerned. 'I hope we didn't push her into talking to us. She only discovered his body yesterday, she'll be in shock.'

'We're best talking to her while it's all fresh in her mind,' reasoned Joyce. 'She might forget things as the reality of what happened starts to sink in and she gets hit by even more emotion. We need her fresh.'

'You make her sound like a slab of meat.'

'I prefer that fresh too.' Joyce shrugged with a slight smile. 'I know, she's a human being. She's also here.'

Joyce waved and Ginger looked over her shoulder. Nancy had a particularly pointy face and was always moving quickly, which made her look like a human arrow. Bustling over, she walked to their table with quick little steps after giving the two women a brief wave. Ginger mused on how perfectly she seemed to fit the role of a housekeeper. Nancy had probably picked up Kenneth's empty cups a nanosecond after he'd placed them on the table, and as he'd told them on Saturday, dust barely had the time to settle. She imagined the woman folding clothing briskly, ensuring pencil-sharp creases.

After a waiter had come to take their order and the three women had each asked for coffee, Nancy opened the conversation.

'Thank you for coming all this way. I don't want to be too far from the house in case the police call and say I can go back in. There will be so much cleaning to do, with the officers tramping their big boots all over the place, and the mail will need sorting. I need to be sure that everyone knows as well, Kenneth was so popular.'

Ginger noted that Nancy had gone from the shock and tears of the day before to practical mode, no doubt keeping herself busy and further emotion at bay for as long as possible. She was still working for Kenneth in one way or another and remained the loyal housekeeper.

After the two women had again expressed their sympathy and asked Nancy how she was doing, and the waiter had returned with their drinks, they started to dig for useful information.

'Have the police said much to you?' Joyce asked as she blew on her coffee.

'No. Well, they questioned me, but I wasn't much use, I'm afraid. I could tell them some of what was missing – they were not the most expensive things Kenneth owned. His desk had been gone through, but I couldn't be sure what was missing from there. It seems the thieves weren't very well informed: there is a painting over the fireplace which is worth a fortune and they left that behind.'

'Were there any fingerprints?' Ginger wasn't hopeful and Nancy shook her head as expected.

'I'd cleaned the day before, so the place was spotless. I always wanted it to be as nice as possible for Kenneth as it wasn't uncommon for him to have guests over with very little warning, so I had to be ready for that. And, of course, like I said on the phone, I had cleaned some of the house yesterday before I realised... well, you know. Anyway, I don't know if that would have helped the police or not: no dust for prints to show up in, or easier to see fingerprints on a clean surface. Who knows? But whoever it was seems to have been wearing gloves, that's what I heard the police say.'

Nancy spoke a little like she moved, quickly and with determination. Ginger hadn't paid a huge amount of attention to her when they had met at Kenneth's, but now she found her fascinating and wondered if the woman ever slowed down and relaxed.

Joyce pulled out the photograph that included Scroop.

'Did Kenneth say much about the other people in this picture?'

'Oh yes. That's Audrey, isn't it? He was going to visit her. I mustn't forget to contact her, tell her about Kenneth.'

Ginger glanced at Joyce, whose eyes had lit up. That was an ideal excuse for dropping by.

'Don't worry about that, we can tell her. We're going to see her too.'

The three women sat in silence for a few minutes, drinking their coffee. It was Ginger who spoke first.

'I know we asked you something similar yesterday, but now you've had more time to think, was Kenneth involved in anything, anything at all, which might have got him killed? Is there anything you heard or saw that made you concerned, other than the business about Scroop?'

Nancy put her cup down. She seemed to be giving the question some thought and looked a little concerned. Had Ginger upset her? She wasn't as quick to respond as she had been yesterday, but that wasn't necessarily suspicious. Perhaps she was just taking the question very seriously.

Finally, Nancy shook her head. 'No. He was a good man,' she said, but her voice lacked the conviction it had held the day before. 'Very particular about certain things, but I liked that. We were similar in that way.'

They descended back into silence until their coffee had been drunk.

'Before I forget,' Joyce piped up, 'does the name Tobias Harrison-Hunt mean anything to you?'

'It does. Kenneth never spoke to me about him directly, but I'm familiar with his name. He visited Kenneth once or twice, but I wasn't there at the time.'

After a beat, Nancy pulled out her phone. Ginger could see that she didn't have any missed calls.

'I should go to the house, they'll probably forget to call me. The police, I mean. I'll go and ask, you never know…'

She stood quickly and gathered up the cardigan she had hung on the back of the chair. 'I don't know why I brought this with me, I won't need it. Well, nice to see you both. I'll contact you when the… well, the arrangements are made.' With that, she scuttled away, the word *funeral* clearly one step too far for her.

'I don't trust her,' Joyce declared as she tapped a long finger-nail against the side of her cup.

'That's a bit harsh. She seemed like she was very loyal to Kenneth.'

'Okay, so maybe that's not what I mean. She didn't tell us the whole truth. How about that, better?'

'Possibly, but what do you mean?'

'When she said that Kenneth wasn't involved in anything else, she didn't jump to his defence, which is what I would have expected of someone as loyal as you say she seems. Which I agree with, actually. But there was something she was hiding. I think we give it a day or two, and then we call her again. No more good cop, good cop; one of us needs to turn the thumbscrews.'

'That's your job then, Joyce. You probably have a collection of thumbscrews and a whole host of torture equipment in your basement.'

Joyce didn't argue.

15

*J*oyce knew there were people who thought she was a clothing-obsessed airhead, but her interest in all things fashion was real and in-depth. She could talk at length about the history of design, and although she had a very sure sense of her own style, she loved seeing what the next generations of artists and designers were coming up with.

It had started with her mother's costumes. The sequins and feathers had caught her child's eye, the work of the designers who took the Tiller Girls around the world and back in time – be they cowgirls, Egyptian queens or military personnel – capturing her imagination, and her interest had grown from there. It wasn't just clothes; Joyce could tell you the origin of a chair design or discuss the influences of Charles Rennie Mackintosh. She had spent a fortune supporting young jewellery designers, which had resulted in a vast earring collection.

The Liberty store in its Tudor revival building, with its history of collaborating with artists and designers, was somewhere she always enjoyed whiling away a few hours. She was planning on surprising Ginger with a trip to the Victoria and Albert museum later in the week, but that could wait. Today, she wanted to add to her hat collection and believed you could never have too many sunglasses.

After her shopping spree, Joyce had found time to drop her bags off at the flat and quickly change into a demure cream summer dress with a brown belt. Being Joyce, however, she topped the outfit off with her new panama hat, to which she had added an animal print scarf as a band. Enormous patterned plastic hoop earrings matching the scarf and stilettos, that would have put the fear of God into any passing leopard, lion or tiger, completed the outfit. The end result was a little *Out of Africa*, but Joyce was satisfied that it wouldn't terrify the old lady they were about to meet. After all, Audrey was no stranger to eye-catching outfits.

'Waterloo, please,' she ordered the driver of the black taxi she had waved over.

'The station?'

'Well, I'm a bit late for the battle.' He spun the taxi round in the road, not bothering with a three-point turn, instead using the tight turning circle London taxis were famous for. Probably annoyed at being pulled over for such a short trip, he executed the manoeuvre a bit too fast for Joyce's liking. He could at least be grateful for the work.

'Where's your spear?' called Ginger as Joyce got out of the taxi. Examining Joyce's earrings, she added, 'And there are some children who would like to have their hula hoops back.'

Joyce touched one of her earrings; maybe she had overdone it slightly. What was she thinking? You could never go too bright or too big.

'For that, you can buy our tickets.'

As they settled back into the train seats, Joyce outlined their plans for when they arrived in Walton-on-Thames.

'We'll get a taxi from the station; it's not far, but in this heat, walking is unnecessary.' Joyce was looking at the map on her phone, having refused the paper map of London that Ginger had thrust in her direction. 'I'll book it now, something you can't do with that thing. There is something to be said for technology, you know.'

'I'm not anti-technology, I just don't want to be surrounded by it all day, every day.'

'Luddite.'

'I'm not *opposed* to technology, although the Luddites were textile workers, so who knows? I might have taken their side back in the day.'

Once Joyce had finished, she gazed out of the window and thought about Audrey Ashmore – or rather, Audrey Valentine as she had been when her mother knew her. Audrey had looked so young in the photograph, it made her angry to think of the way she had been treated by Scroop. Joyce had never met her, but she was expecting a demure, small-framed lady who, hopefully, could throw some light on Kenneth's recent activities, maybe even on who might have wanted him dead.

Informing Audrey that Kenneth had passed was one job that Joyce was not looking forward to, but getting involved with something like murder was going to throw up some unpleasant jobs. It wasn't completely odd that she should be the bearer of the bad news; after all, her mother had been a friend and confidante to Audrey in the past. Joyce was, however, very pleased that Ginger was with her. If Joyce couldn't find the words, Ginger would be able to. She exuded warmth in a way that Joyce knew she lacked. Well, unless breathing fire counted.

Audrey lived in a large detached house on a very nice street. Joyce guessed the house was worth well over a million pounds; it seemed far too large for one elderly lady and Joyce wondered if Audrey lived with her family, or they with her. There was a gleaming motorcycle on the driveway and she doubted that Audrey was the owner, although perhaps she shouldn't be so quick to judge. Joyce herself planned on living life to the fullest until she was 101, at which point she was going to snuff it while dining at the Savoy with a glass of very expensive champagne in her hand. Although motorbikes weren't her thing right now, if she changed her mind, then no one would stop her, no matter what her age.

She was about to ring the bell when Ginger brought her attention to an open gate at the side of the house. They followed the path around to the back. In the middle of a large, well-kept lawn was an enormous umbrella, within its shade a collection of comfortable wicker garden furniture and one elderly lady, her nose buried in a book. She wore a light-blue summer dress and her face was framed by waves of soft white hair.

Joyce and Ginger made their way slowly across the grass, not wanting to give the woman a heart attack.

'Audrey?' Joyce said, cautiously. The woman looked up; there was nothing wrong with her hearing.

'Yes.'

'My name is Joyce, Joyce Brocklehurst. You used to dance with my mother Margaret.'

Audrey leant forward and squinted, examining the tall woman who, from her point of view, must have seemingly appeared from nowhere.

'Well I never, you're Margaret Brocklehurst's girl. Well, one of them. I don't know what to say; this is a surprise.' She started to rise from her chair.

'Please, don't get up. This is my friend, Ginger Salt. Do you mind if we join you?'

'I'd be most offended if you didn't. Please take a seat. What a wonderful surprise.'

Joyce felt a mixture of great pleasure at connecting with one of her mother's old dance friends and dread at what she had to tell Audrey.

'My son is around here somewhere. When he comes out, I'll ask him to get some drinks for us. I made a jug of lemonade this morning and it will be nice and cool now. To what do I owe this pleasure? I do miss your mother, she was such a wonderful, determined woman, I really looked up to her. She was also very, very kind to me.'

Joyce had folded herself demurely into her chair. Despite her mother having passed away many years ago, she felt the need to make a good impression on Margaret's friend. It was an unfamiliar feeling, like being a young girl again, knowing that she should behave and not wanting to say anything inappropriate. For a brief moment, she wondered if perhaps her mother knew where she was and who she was with.

She realised that Audrey and Ginger were looking at her. Audrey smiled and rested a small, delicate hand on Joyce's arm. Perhaps she knew what Joyce had been thinking.

'And Ginger? Is that right? Are you a dancer?'

Joyce stifled a laugh.

'No, although I used to work in the theatre, in the wardrobe department for various companies.'

'Oh, how marvellous! I used to love the costumes. There couldn't be too many sequins or feathers. Although some of those headdresses were a bit precarious. Now, I sense there is a reason you ladies are both here, so please…'

Audrey's attention was drawn to a man with fine ginger hair who was walking across the lawn from the house.

'Oh, Robert, come and meet my friends. This is my son. Robert, this is Joyce and Ginger.' The man, who appeared to be in his late fifties, stooped under the umbrella and shook their hands.

'I didn't hear anyone arrive. Nice to meet you.'

'I used to dance with Joyce's mother. We were about to do

some reminiscing. Would you mind fetching us some lemonade from the fridge?'

Robert smiled kindly at his mother. 'Of course, and can I get you ladies anything to eat?' It hadn't escaped Joyce's attention that he was rather handsome. He looked as if he took care of himself and those fingernails had experienced a manicure. He wasn't wearing a wedding ring either.

Ginger shook her head.

'Not for me, thank you,' replied Joyce, smiling as sweetly as she could.

'One jug of lemonade coming up.'

'Nice motorbike, by the way,' Joyce said, knowing that men often liked to have their chrome toys complimented. Robert looked momentarily confused, and then laughed in recognition.

'Oh, that's my dad's. We still haven't been able to bring ourselves to sell it. I pull it out from time to time to give it a polish. I think I'm the only man in the family who doesn't have an interest in two wheels. Mum's not keen, are you?'

Audrey gave an exaggerated look of horror. 'Every time my grandson gets on his, I worry. Most of the time, I don't want to know.'

'You know he's careful, Mum,' said Robert, the warmth in his voice reassuring. He smiled again, then strode purposefully back across the lawn.

'Now, where were we? Oh yes, you were going to tell me to what I owe the honour of this lovely surprise visit.'

Joyce glanced at Ginger before speaking. 'Do you remember Kenneth Gaddy? He was around when you knew my mother.'

'Of course I do. Kenneth is a lovely man. I haven't seen him for a while, but Robert has contact with him now and again.'

That surprised Joyce and she made a note to follow it up.

'I'm sorry, Audrey, but he passed away the other day.'

'Oh my, I'm so sorry to hear that. He was a good man. You know, he left a phone message for me the other week and I never got round to returning his call. Oh, I do feel bad now; we should never put things off until tomorrow. I do hope he slipped away peacefully.'

'I'm afraid not. I'm sorry, Audrey, but he was murdered.'

Audrey stared at Joyce, her mouth open as though she was about to speak, but no words came out. Eventually, she turned away.

'Poor Kenneth,' she whispered. 'Poor, poor Kenneth.'

---

16

*G*inger had opted to remain a bystander. There was a tie between Joyce and Audrey that she didn't have, and until the reference to Kenneth's death, she had been enjoying watching Joyce connect with her mother's friend. She could see how much it meant to Audrey too and it was lovely to watch the two women together. But it was only a matter of time until the conversation had needed to take a gloomy and upsetting turn.

There had been a brief moment of silence as Audrey had taken in the news. She had dabbed at her eyes with a handkerchief that had been tucked between her and the chair.

'What happened, do you know?'

'The police think it was a break-in,' Joyce explained.

Audrey appeared to be thinking, and then turned quickly to face Joyce. 'But you don't think it was, do you?' Joyce looked surprised. 'I might be old, but my hearing is one thing that has yet to leave me and there was something in the way you said that. *They* think, *you* don't. Is that why you're here?'

Joyce didn't have a chance to respond as Robert was returning, a tray in his hands with a large jug and three glasses. The lemonade was full of ice and it looked wonderful. He started to pour the drinks.

'Robert, dear, Joyce has just informed me that Kenneth Gaddy has passed. Had you heard anything about this?' The lemonade he was pouring went over the edge of the glass and onto the table. He put the jug down, but didn't look at his mother.

'Heavens, no, nothing. When did it happen?' He looked at Ginger, then Joyce. 'How did you find out?'

Ginger was the one to reply. 'He died on Sunday. We visited him on Saturday when we first arrived in London, so we were two of the last people to see him alive and the police wanted to talk to us.'

It took him a second or two to respond. 'Why the police?'

'He was murdered, Robert,' Audrey said.

'Oh my God. How? What happened?'

'We're not sure, the police are on the case though,' said Ginger. Audrey reached over and put a hand on Robert's arm.

'You'll need to let the rest of the committee know, if they haven't found out already.'

'Yes, yes, of course, Mother. I'll phone Malcolm straight away. Kenneth was due to host a dinner for key fundraisers next month, so we'll need to discuss that.' He had finished pouring the drinks as his mother spoke, his hand steadier now. 'Let me know if you'd like more.' He left the women to it and returned to the house.

'What was that about a committee?' Ginger asked, feeling that was territory she was happy to venture into.

'Kenneth and Robert are both trustees for a contemporary dance company based in Spitalfields. Kenneth had been involved for a number of years and Robert joined because they needed someone with financial expertise. Robert is an accountant, but he has always had a passion for the arts and dances as a hobby. He gets that from both his father and me. As a result, he had more contact with Kenneth than me.'

'Do you know why Kenneth was trying to contact you?'

'No, I don't. Oh, I do wish I had called him back. I kept thinking that it could wait. We last spoke properly at an opening night last year. Robert was always offering to take me to see the company perform. I used to go more regularly, but I find getting about harder these days and it's so exhausting to travel into London, even if Robert drives, so I rarely venture in anymore. But it was last September. That's right, an American choreographer had come over to work with the dance company and Robert was very keen for me to join him. Kenneth was there and was wonderful company. That was the last time I saw him. I'm afraid I have reached that age where your circle of friends gets gradually smaller and smaller. Although you don't expect they'll go like this.'

She stared off into the distance. Ginger wondered if it was time to leave her alone with her thoughts, but Joyce wasn't finished.

'Audrey, I want to ask you something.'

'Of course, anything. What would you like to know?'

'It's about Scroop, Scroop Harrison de Clare.'

There was no shift in the expression on Audrey's face. She remained composed, but Ginger was sure she could see her take a deep breath.

'What about him?'

'I'm sorry, you've probably tried to forget him, but have you any idea what happened to him? Who wanted to kill him?'

Audrey glanced down at her hands and slowly twisted her wedding band.

'You're probably aware that Scroop was not a good man. He was handsome and could be charming, when he wanted to be. But deep down, he was very unpleasant. It would often take people a long time to realise this, but realise they did, and as a result there were many who didn't shed a tear when he was killed. I will be honest with you, I was amongst them. I was relieved. But did I know who hated him enough to want to kill him? No.

'I did wonder if someone had been pushed too far and just snapped, or it was an accident or self-defence. But after a while, I stopped wondering and moved on. We all did – your mother, Kenneth, all of our friends. After we got over the shock that someone we knew had been killed, we never talked of him again.'

During the silence that followed, Ginger knew that it was time to leave and she tapped Joyce gently on the arm. Joyce nodded.

'We should be going. Audrey, I'm sorry that we had to meet under these circumstances.'

'Oh, please don't be sorry. I'm just so pleased I got to see Margaret's girl. Promise me you'll say hello if you're in the area again.'

Joyce took her hand and gave it a squeeze. 'Of course.'

They both kissed Audrey and said goodbye. None of these people – Kenneth, Jim, Audrey – had previously played any part in Ginger's life, but even she had been hit by a feeling of sadness. For once, she desperately wanted to be back in the busy city, distracted by the hustle and bustle.

They walked back to the station in silence.

17

'There's a half bottle of Moët in the fridge, would you be a darling and pop it open?'

Joyce needed a drink and the thought of a glass of champagne had kept her going on the train ride back into London. She had desperately wanted to spend more time with Audrey talking about her mother, but it hadn't been the right moment for that. She was, however, pleased she had been able to tell her about Kenneth face to face; that Audrey hadn't found out via an email sent to Robert by the chair of the trustees or whoever. That, she was sure, her mother would have been grateful for as well.

By the time Joyce returned from powdering her nose, Ginger had two glasses of champagne poured and was standing on the balcony.

'Madam.' Ginger curtseyed as she handed over one of the glasses.

'If you were my maid, you wouldn't be sharing it with me.'

'If I was your maid… well, I wouldn't be your maid because I'd have quit after an hour.'

Joyce considered a comeback, and then laughed. 'You're probably right. I'd have a revolving door of staff.'

They took their first sips looking out over the Thames. A speedboat full of tourists shot past; the sound of drinkers from down below in the Founder's Arms pub travelled up to them. The dome of St. Paul's Cathedral stood strong against the background of the blue sky.

'Okay, we have an hour to don our glad rags. I've booked us a table for dinner at an Italian restaurant, and then we're going to the Gilmore Club.'

'Ooh, fancy. And what's so special about the Gilmore Club?' Ginger's eyes had lit up.

You have to give her her due, thought Joyce, *she is up for trying anything new, even if she has no idea what she is about to try.*

'When I was digging up some information on Tobias Harrison-Hunt, relative of the charming-sounding Scroop, I saw that he is holding some kind of book event at the Gilmore Club this evening. It's in conjunction with a whisky distiller. It's a members' only club, so we're going to have to charm our way in. It's also the club that my boss goes to, but I'm not aware that he's in London at the moment so we won't run into him.'

'Can't you give him a call, get us on a guest list?'

'We're not talking about the manager of a supermarket here; he's the Duke of Ravensbury, head of one of the most high-ranking aristocratic families in the country.'

'And you're Joyce Brocklehurst, head of retail in the aforementioned Duke's home, and not exactly backwards at coming forwards.'

'True, but it's still a no. We'll find a way in. Just put all your best assets on show, follow my lead and before you know it, we'll be sipping a dram and pretending to enjoy whatever tedious dirge of a book Tobias is talking about.'

'I'm not much of a fan of whisky, I'd rather have a bourbon.'

'You are for one night. You never know, I might find myself a rich husband.'

'And I a rich wife?'

'If you behave yourself and don't screw your nose up when offered a peaty dram, then very possibly.' Joyce topped up their glasses, and then left Ginger to it. She was laying claim to the bathroom.

'How do I look?'

Joyce gave a slow, delicate twirl, showing off the long red dress she had opted to wear for the evening. The hem reached her ankles, the split reached high on her thigh and the neckline plunged... and plunged. It was close fitting, but unusually for Joyce, it wasn't *too* closely fitted. It was elegant, yet simultaneously left little to the imagination.

A multi-coloured chiffon scarf hung loosely around her shoulders, her hair formed a tidy bun and she wore a pair of red stilettos with toe points that could spear fish. Each fingernail had been painted a different colour, each one matching a colour on her scarf. This final touch was pure Joyce. When she had once been asked if she bled in rainbow colours, she'd responded that her blood knew to match whatever outfit she was wearing that day.

'Are you not a tad overdressed?' asked Ginger as she hurriedly pulled on her shoes.

'I can always say we are going on to a party afterwards. We can't risk being underdressed or we'll never get in. Come on, show me...'

Ginger spun around. She had opted for a silk trouser suit that Joyce knew she had made herself. Once again, she found herself wowed by Ginger's skills. The burgundy trousers and loose cream boat-neck top made a flattering combination, her jewellery was the exact same shade as the trousers, and her cream ballet shoes gave the outfit a delicate touch. There were no obvious signs of makeup, which Ginger didn't need as she had perfect skin, and her silver hair had been pinned up neatly.

'Why you don't have a wife already, I'll never know,' Joyce said harshly, but she could see from Ginger's face that she took it for the compliment it was intended to be.

18

After eating their dinner cautiously to ensure the sauce didn't drip on their outfits, Joyce and Ginger made their way to Pall Mall, a central London street notorious for its private clubs in grand buildings with Doric and Corinthian columns. Behind the doors were ostentatious displays of wealth and, typically, masculinity. Grand staircases; ornate dining rooms; lounges and bars full of leather and deep 'manly' colours; wine cellars worth the same as a small nation's annual GDP – all for the enjoyment of members who could afford the exorbitant fees (after having sat patiently on a waiting list for years) and their lucky guests.

Many of the clubs had opened their membership to women, but the Gilmore Club had stuck to its guns and women were only permitted as guests of members. This archaic attitude meant that Ginger was in a bad mood before they'd even crossed the threshold.

'Bloody Neanderthals. It's hard to believe they can still get away with it. They're only showing themselves up as the arrogant, pig-headed...'

Joyce fired a glare her way. They were about to walk through the door, so Ginger clammed up. She would fume quietly to herself. They were here on a mission and once that had been completed, they could head to a bar full of sane people. After a strong drink, she'd return to the flat and take a shower, cleanse herself of the overpoweringly toxic...

Ginger's thoughts were brought to a rapid halt by the sight of the room they had walked into. The lobby of the club was a large marble-decked space, columns on all sides supporting a wide balcony. Above that, a vast glass dome threw light into the space. Large portraits covered the walls, and directly beyond them, through the columns, was a grand staircase that wouldn't have looked out of place on the *Titanic*. She was immediately relieved they had made such an effort with their outfits.

She heard a cough behind them.

'Good evening, ladies, can I be of assistance?' The man who had walked out from behind a desk was so perfectly put together that he seemed a little unreal. Trimmed grey hair that looked as though you could lift it off in one piece; a smart waistcoat and jacket which didn't have a detail out of place; a tie that appeared to have been knotted with a ruler to hand so that it was exactly symmetrical; and a name badge which must have required a spirit level to get it so straight.

Joyce brought her shoulders back, took a step forward and towered over him. He didn't flinch.

'Good evening... Elliot. We're here to attend the Tobias Harrison-Hunt event.'

'Of course, madam. Do you have your invitations?'

'We certainly do.' Joyce pretended to root around her small red handbag before letting out a slightly embarrassed laugh. 'Silly me, I put them on the dressing table and forgot to pick them up as I left. We did receive them, however, I assure you.'

'And who are you guests of?'

'I beg your pardon?'

'Which member sent you the invitation, madam? Only members and their guests can attend.'

Joyce paused before looking at Ginger.

'Was it William or Fairfax who sent them, my dear? I can't remember.'

Ginger shook her head.

'I honestly don't recall, although the Earl of Cottingham said he would send us an invitation. It might have been to this event.'

'Earl of Cottingham?' Elliot raised an eyebrow. Ginger knew they'd been rumbled, but at least he had the decency to return to his desk and pretend to look at the book in front of him, running his fingers down the list of guests. 'I'm afraid we don't have an Earl of Cottingham in this evening; might it be someone else?'

There was a pause as the two women looked at one another.

'Might we just go and take a look?' asked Joyce as she started to walk towards a doorway. 'I'm sure I'll be able to see William or Fairfax and they'll vouch for us.'

Elliot stepped out from behind the desk again and placed himself in front of the door just before Joyce reached it, her hand outstretched.

'I'm afraid you can't go any further without a member to escort you, and that's the cloakroom.'

'Elliot, my good man, I am impressed by how diligently you are performing your duties and I will be sure to pass that on to my associates. Now if there is any chance...'

Ginger watched as Joyce reached into her bag and started to pull out what looked like a £20 note.

'Elliot, good evening. I believe you have met my guests.' The strong, confident voice made them all turn around. 'Joyce, how wonderful to see you, I'm very pleased you could make it. And... and... yes, marvellous to see you too. I'll sign them in, Elliot.'

Ginger smiled and looked over at Joyce. Fortunately, Joyce wore so much makeup, it wasn't possible to see the distinct shade of red that Ginger was convinced would be travelling up her face.

Joyce gave a slight nod at their rescuer.

'Your Grace, it was very kind of you to invite us.' Her voice was a little less certain than usual; Ginger wasn't used to seeing Joyce on the back foot. It seemed that Joyce's certainty that her employer, the Duke of Ravensbury, was not currently visiting London had been misplaced, but that turned out to be a good thing.

'Ladies, if you'd like to come with me, I'd be honoured to escort you to the bar.' The Duke indicated towards the stairs. Joyce smiled and walked forward with a spring in her step; it looked as though at least some of her confidence had returned.

19

*A*lexander Fitzwilliam-Scott, the 12th Duke of Ravensbury, returned to the table with their drinks. There was no denying that he was a handsome man. Slim with silver-grey hair, a patrician nose and way of carrying himself that spoke of his confidence, style and influence, he was clearly at ease in their rarefied surroundings. He was wearing a smart blue suit with a pale-blue tie. His clothing was understated, but so beautifully cut to his figure that you'd know instinctively it was very expensive.

'Joyce, this is an unexpected… well, I hesitate to say pleasure until I find out why you were trying to talk your way into one of the country's most exclusive clubs. It is, however, most definitely unexpected.'

'There is a talk we want to attend and we simply couldn't miss it.'

'It must be a very good talk. Who is it that's… do you mean the Tobias Harrison-Hunt event? Why on earth would you be interested in him? And I can't quite picture you as a whisky drinker.'

Joyce looked at Ginger, who gave a little shrug. She appeared to be enjoying this.

'I have a long-held interest in… in…' Joyce mumbled something as she raised her glass to her lips.

'You have no idea what his book's about, do you…'

'The scientific achievements of the Ottoman Empire,' Joyce blurted out, much more loudly than she'd intended, having remembered the focus of one of Tobias's previous books. The Duke smiled, although it looked a little like a smirk, if he would lower himself to such a thing.

'Well remembered, Joyce! Although this talk is actually about the role of his family in the First World War. If you believed what he wrote, you'd think his family singlehandedly won the blasted thing for us.'

There was silence. It was Ginger who dared break it with the obvious statement.

'It sounds like you're not keen on him.'

'Hmm, you might say that. May I ask why you are really interested in him? And please, only the truth now, otherwise I might have to rescind my invitation for you to join me here as a guests.' There was humour in his eyes as he peered over his glass at the two women, but Joyce knew this was no longer the time for games. She put her glass down.

'We're interested in an incident that happened some years ago. A relative of Tobias knew my mother. That relative, Scroop Harrison de Clare, was murdered many years ago and we were wondering if Tobias could shed any light onto what happened.'

The Duke stared at them for what felt like an interminably long time. He looked a little like a contender for the role of James Bond in his later years; he certainly had the style and confidence. Eventually, he spoke.

'I'm guessing this is nothing but innocent curiosity?' He clearly didn't expect an answer. 'Alright, I'm going to assume, Joyce, this is nothing more than research into your family history and you're not doing anything that could get you into trouble.'

He gave Joyce a look which made it clear he was being extremely serious. 'I'm not prone to gossip, but I would hate to think of you getting mixed up in anything that would be... bad for you, either through losing money or something else. The entire family has a reputation for being somewhat ruthless. Charming, yes, but that's really just an act. I've made a point of not getting involved in their business affairs and being no more than an acquaintance, and you'll find that the longer-serving members of the club take the same approach. We've been here long enough to understand what Tobias and his family are really like.'

'Are we just talking shady business deals, or is it more than that?' asked Ginger. The Duke looked at her and seemed to consider his answer, not replying immediately. He placed his glass on the table.

'The problem is, when things become... *shady,* to use your word, it's often impossible to prove the matter being discussed. People know, or at least have a feeling they know what's going on, but the evidence is hard to find, especially if those concerned are clever. And that family consists of a lot of very intelligent people. It is simply best to stay away.

'Tobias can be good company, there is no denying that. He is, as I say, charming; he can even come across as kind and considerate. He's raised a great deal of money for charity, but even that is more about his own profile and reputation. If you wish to discuss old family connections, I'm sure that will be fine, but I suggest you leave it at that. Now, my appointment has arrived, and Tobias's talk seems to have finished.'

Joyce looked across the room to see a very tall man with a military bearing, and what was no doubt a wig, acknowledge the Duke. Behind him, a number of people were filtering into the room, whisky glasses in their hands.

The Duke stood. 'This has been an unexpected...' he paused, and then smiled, '...pleasure. Please, enjoy the rest of your evening, ladies, and put any drinks on my tab.'

'I'm not a whole lot clearer on what the risks around Tobias are, he didn't actually tell us much,' said Ginger as she watched the Duke walk over to his acquaintance.

'He's the Duke of Ravensbury and we're in his club. He can't say much; he doesn't want to get involved in some bust-up with Tobias for slander.'

'I'm surprised you didn't try and seduce a bit more out of him.'

'Give over, he's my boss and so is his wife. I know I like a good time, but I'm not going to risk my job. Right, that's him, Tobias. It's time to go in for the kill.'

'Be careful. Remember what the Duke said.'

'I will and I'm not doing it alone. Come on.'

20

*T*obias Harrison-Hunt had a soft, fleshy look which gave him a boyish appearance, but Ginger decided he was probably somewhere in his forties. His dark blazer had been matched with a stripy tie which screamed of private schools and a desire to be included. He had a laugh that was a touch too loud and gestures which were a touch too dramatic. This was a man who liked to be the centre of attention.

It was a matter of seconds before Joyce caught his eye. Ginger had been wondering how long that would take and hoped that he had a thing for older women. He turned to face them and smiled.

Joyce stepped forward. 'Excellent talk, deeply fascinating. You're clearly dedicated to your work.'

'Thank you, that's very kind.' He took a moment to take in the two women. 'I have to confess that I don't recall seeing you in there.'

'We popped in at the last minute and didn't want to put you off your flow. Didn't we, Ginger?'

Ginger smiled, enjoying the show. Joyce was using her 'lady of the manor' voice and certainly sounded like someone who belonged in a private members' club, even if she was only allowed in as a guest (something which was still irritating Ginger). Joyce was standing tall and had ensured that two of her best assets were front and centre. Following his gaze, Ginger could tell they were doing their job well and Tobias was struggling to maintain eye contact with her.

'Well, you were very discreet; I wasn't at all aware of your arrival. Can I get you both a drink?'

'That would be lovely, and then we would rather like a chat.'

He looked surprised by that, but nodded with an expression of bemused curiosity on his face. Ginger guessed he was unlikely to turn down the company of such a striking woman as Joyce and she was happy to play second fiddle. Joyce had a job to do and, dressed like that, she was going to get that job done. It didn't matter, to Ginger at least, that this was a rather obvious and some might call it 'cheap' way of doing it; they wanted answers and would do anything within the law to get them.

After ordering drinks, Tobias led them to a table in a far corner of the bar and they all sank into the deep leather armchairs. The chairs' high backs provided a level of privacy, which Ginger was sure many of the members were extremely grateful for.

'I'm curious,' began Tobias, 'who are you the guests of?'

'His Grace the Duke of Ravensbury,' replied Ginger, enjoying the opportunity to make such a statement. She wasn't one to kowtow to nobility, but it certainly felt good to be able to name someone quite so significant. Tobias was clearly taken aback, but tried not to let it show too much and reined himself in with a nod.

'Good man, very good man. We're close to some quite significant business deals, he and I; there are a few small points to iron out and, of course, these things often take time, but he was very keen for us to join forces on one or two things… So, you enjoy my books?'

Another wave of satisfaction travelled through Ginger. She

knew he was lying and it felt rather good to be aware of that. She noted that he'd changed the subject quickly; he wouldn't want them asking questions about these imaginary business deals. It was risky enough that he would make those statements to people who clearly knew the Duke.

'Immensely,' confirmed Joyce.

Ginger nodded along, then asked, 'Is it true that you are in the midst of writing another book about your family?'

'It is – how did you know about that?'

The two women glanced at one another, then Ginger mumbled something through a mouthful of drink about having overheard it. He seemed to accept her non-response.

'Many of my family's achievements are not particularly well known. We're not the type to seek the limelight, but I do think it's time that more of them came out into the open. Now that I have written about our military achievements and ensured some of my ancestors receive the credit they deserve, it's time to talk about a few others.'

'Scroop Harrison de Clare, for example?' Joyce was leaning forward in her chair and doing a good job of feigning a heartfelt fascination. Tobias held her gaze for a moment, but Joyce didn't flinch. 'I believe he was particularly well-known for his philanthropy within the theatre world.'

That seemed to make Tobias relax. 'Yes, yes, that's right. How interesting that you're familiar with him. Yes, extremely generous: many notable musicals were largely funded by him in the early 1950s. It's certainly time that he was given the credit he truly deserves.' But he didn't sound quite as enthusiastic as his words suggested, which confused Ginger. She decided it was time to chip in again.

'It's such a shame that if people know anything about him, it's typically his unfortunate demise,' she said. 'It must be very hard for the family, knowing that his killer was never brought to justice. I'm assuming that there have been no further developments over the years?'

'No, no, there haven't. Why would you be interested in that?'

'Morbid curiosity, I'm afraid. I used to work in London theatre so I have always been aware of the tragic event.' Only the first part was true; Ginger had never heard of the man until Kenneth had talked about him. 'It would be interesting if, during the course of your research, you were to find out who killed him.'

Tobias was starting to eye her with suspicion. Joyce had sat back, clearly letting Ginger see how far she could take this.

'It's interesting that such a well-regarded man would have someone who wanted to kill him. Perhaps you'll be able to discover the truth.' Now, Tobias was looking distinctly less relaxed. 'Have you come across anyone who might have had reason to do him harm?'

Tobias looked at Joyce, but saw a woman as eager as Ginger to find out more.

'Who did you say you are?'

'We're friends of the Duke of Ravensbury,' replied Joyce. 'I have some connections with the theatre world myself: Scroop and my mother were friends.'

A smile began to reappear on Tobias's face. *A moment of misplaced relief*, thought Ginger.

'She knew him at the time he was killed. They were both part of a circle of friends that included Kenneth Gaddy, Sheridan Knight and Audrey Valentine.'

That seemed to change things entirely for Tobias. He clearly recognised those names and it worried him. He held Joyce in what could only be described as a glare, until he remembered himself and smiled a rather horrible forced smile.

'And you're here talking to me because...?'

'Because you might know more about what happened between those people. One of them died recently in suspicious circumstances and we would like to find out more.'

'Who has died?'

'Kenneth.'

That clearly surprised him. 'But I was with him only the other day, he seemed perfectly fine.'

'You were with him?' Now Ginger was surprised.

'Yes, I bought a painting from him. We had coffee in Mayfair and exchanged it there; it wasn't a particularly large painting. How did he die?'

Ginger couldn't be sure, but the way he asked the question was rather flat, as though he already knew the answer. But she was well aware that might be her imagination trying to find reasons to be suspicious.

'He was murdered.'

Tobias remained quiet for a moment, then spoke with a soft tone. 'That is truly dreadful, I hope they catch whoever did it.'

There was another pause until Joyce spoke. 'May I ask, who was the painting by?'

'Which painting?'

'The one you bought from Kenneth.'

'It was by a surrealist called José Antonio Cozar. My family have collected his work for years and Kenneth had one which he was prepared to sell to me.'

'Did you talk about Scroop while you were making the sale?' asked Ginger.

'Why would we do that?'

'You have been doing research on Scroop's life. I believe you've visited at least one London theatre as part of that work, and Kenneth was an associate of his.'

Another flicker of surprise crossed his face and for the first time, he looked truly uncertain. But he soon regained his composure, draining his glass before looking at his watch.

'Ladies, it has been very nice meeting you, but there are a number of people here who wish to discuss this evening's talk with me.'

Ginger waited until he was out of earshot to voice her thoughts.

'If he's really doing research into Scroop, why didn't he ask you about your mother and her connections to his great-uncle, or anything else you might have found out?'

Joyce was watching him as he walked across the room and her gaze never shifted, even when he turned and looked back at her. Tobias joined a group on the far side of the room, but he couldn't stop glancing their way. He really didn't look happy.

'And the purchase of the picture?' asked Ginger. 'Do you think that was as innocent as it sounded?'

Joyce nodded. 'Kenneth loved paintings and antiques – you saw that at his house. He still bought and sold. What I don't understand is if Kenneth was dealing with Tobias, why didn't he have more answers about Scroop's death?'

'Perhaps he asked too many awkward questions during the process of the sale and Tobias decided he had to keep him quiet to protect his family's reputation.' This whole angle was confusing, but it also created a few possibilities, one of them being that Kenneth had pushed Tobias too far and died as a result.

'Come on, Ginger, I think it's time we went. We got what we came for.'

'Did we? I don't feel like things are any clearer.'

'*Au contraire*, my friend. Tobias Harrison-Hunt is very concerned that we might know something about his great-uncle, something he'd rather the world didn't know.'

Ginger wondered if Tobias was capable of killing an old man and took another look at him. He had the strength and he could have had the opportunity. After all, if he was a full-time writer, he had his own schedule, and he had the excuse of the artwork to get inside Kenneth's house. Yes, if he wanted to keep a few family skeletons firmly in the closet, murder might have been the only way to do it.

21

'I want to know more about that artwork,' Ginger said as they made their way to the door of the bar. 'It might be important enough to kill for.'

'But he bought it, he didn't need to kill for it.'

'No, not this time, but there's always shenanigans in the art world. Valuable pieces going missing; people spending their family fortunes on tracking down some rare artefact that turns out not to exist anyway.'

'You've been watching too many heist films.'

'You can't watch too many heist films.' Ginger looked at her as though the idea was utterly ridiculous.

Joyce sighed. 'Alright. I know who might be able to help and we don't have to leave the building.' She steered them back across the room in the direction of the Duke of Ravensbury and his companion. The Duke spotted Joyce before they reached him, which wasn't hard to do, and stood.

'Ladies, I hope your conversation with Tobias was useful.'

'Reasonably so,' replied Joyce. 'I'm sorry to disturb you, but you might be able to help us.'

'If I can, I'd be delighted.'

Joyce caught the eye of the other man. He had remained seated, but was giving her more than just a once-over. Despite the wig, he wasn't bad looking; he looked like an extra from an episode of *Downton Abbey* in a slightly more modern suit.

She turned and focused on the Duke. 'I know you enjoy art.'

'You could say that, our collection at Charleton House isn't too bad.' The sarcasm dripped off his words. A price couldn't be put on the private collection his family owned; it was one of the finest in the country.

'Have you heard of José Antonio Cozar?'

'Of course, surrealist. Never given the credit he deserved and died far too young. We used to own one, but my father sold it, sadly. Why are you interested in Cozar?'

'Because Tobias Harrison-Hunt is interested.'

The Duke appeared to ponder that statement, and then smiled.

'Of course, he's on a quest. The family collected Cozar's work for a long time, but Scroop wasn't a fan and, despite not needing the money, sold a number of his paintings to invest in some of his little projects. I'm told his mother was furious.'

'So the family would be very keen to get the paintings back?'

The Duke laughed. 'It's been the pet project of Tobias and his brother for years. They'd exchange their own grandmother for one of those paintings.'

Joyce could see Ginger smiling. That was exactly the kind of information they needed.

'Thank you, Your Grace.'

'That was useful?'

'Very. Thank you again for your help this evening, enjoy the rest of your night.'

'Thank *you*, Joyce. I'll see you back at Charleton soon, I'm sure.' He gave a slight nod of his head, said goodnight to Ginger and sat down. Joyce led Ginger from the room, but not before she'd heard the Duke's friend comment on her being *rather fine* and did he have her phone number? Joyce smiled to herself: she hadn't lost her touch.

As they stepped out onto the street, Joyce's phone beeped. It was a bit late for anyone to be contacting her, but she took the call, ignoring Ginger as she mouthed *'Who is it?'* at her.

'Right, to bed,' she said as she ended the brief conversation. 'Let's get some beauty sleep before an early start tomorrow. That was Nancy – she wants to meet us for coffee again first thing.'

*a*t 8am, Joyce and Ginger were back at Hampstead Heath. The glorious blue skies of the last couple of days had been replaced with cloud cover, but it was still warm enough for them to sit outside.

'Have you any idea what she might want?' Ginger asked as they chose their seats and made themselves comfortable. Joyce shook her head.

'She might have been allowed back in the house and found something that worries her, and perhaps she doesn't wish to tell the police. Not everyone is comfortable dealing with our boys in blue. I, of course, would welcome the opportunity to converse with a man in uniform. I'll never understand how some people aren't attracted to…'

'Joyce, focus! If you need a man in uniform, we can head to Horse Guards Parade later and kidnap a member of the mounted regiment. I'm not sure what we'll do with his horse, but we'll think of something.'

Their banter was interrupted by the sight of Nancy walking over to join them. She looked worried.

'Sorry to drag you all the way out here again, I really am. I just knew I needed to talk to you and if I didn't arrange to do it soon, I'd lose my nerve.'

'Not a problem, we're early risers,' Ginger lied. She could be, but that morning, Ginger could happily have stayed in bed until lunchtime. 'Have the police allowed you back in the house?'

Nancy nodded. 'Yesterday afternoon. There was so much tidying and cleaning to do, I was at it until late last night. All day I was thinking, I couldn't help it, and, well, it got a bit much and I went home and had a couple of glasses of wine and that's when I decided to phone you and…'

Ginger placed a hand on top of Nancy's in an attempt to calm her down and get her to stop talking. 'Take a deep breath.' A couple of dogs ran past their table, their leads dragging behind them as Ginger waited for Nancy to regain her composure. 'Just start at the beginning and tell us – slowly – what it is that's on your mind. There's no rush, we've got all day.' Joyce had actually told Ginger she wanted to go for a manicure as soon as they were done, but she could wait.

'I'm worried about my Matt, I'm afraid he's done something stupid.'

There was a pause. Ginger sighed to herself; she'd said slowly, but she was going to have to get Nancy moving a little more rapidly than this or their conversation was going to take all day. Joyce could only hide her impatience for a limited period of time.

'And Matt is?'

'My grandson. He's twenty-six, but he's really struggled to make his way in life. He and Kenneth got on very well. Kenneth would pay him to do odd jobs in the garden or if he needed some heavy lifting doing – moving furniture, other odd jobs. Matt's unemployed; he tries, but he's not found anything that interests him. He's a bright lad, just a bit… well, easily distracted.'

Ginger knew right away what Nancy meant. Matt was a lazy

good-for-nothing, but his grandmother's love wouldn't allow her to say that.

'Kenneth helped him out sometimes: lent him money, that kind of thing, even though he knew he'd never get it back. He let Matt stay in the guest room a few times when his parents had kicked him out.' She stopped and looked at the two women sitting in front of her. 'He's a good lad really, it wasn't his fault. He wasn't a hardened addict, said the drugs were his way of *chilling out.* Kenneth talked to him about getting help and put him in touch with people, and it seemed to work. After that, he was on and off them, but it never seemed serious. We – Kenneth and me – we both thought it was, what's the word? *Recreational.* He was still the same Matt – *is* the same Matt. Great sense of humour. We have film nights and he turns up with ice cream and popcorn; we both really like a good, silly comedy.'

Nancy perked up as she described their evenings together and pulled a photo of a young man out of her handbag, handing it to Ginger. He was good-looking, but the smirk on his face and lazy slouch in his overall bearing made him less appealing.

Out of the corner of her eye, Ginger could see Joyce's fingers start to twitch. If they didn't get a new layer of some lurid nail polish in the next few hours, they might end up smashing a blunt object into some unfortunate's head. Then Ginger rebuked herself for thinking that. It was a bit too close to what had happened to Kenneth.

'Nancy, what is it about Matt that's got you so worried right now?' she asked.

Nancy sighed and looked at the photo that Ginger had returned before putting it back in her bag.

'He asked Kenneth for some money and Kenneth said no. I think he'd finally had enough. They argued about it; I was in the kitchen and heard it all. I was about to go in and try to calm things down when Matt stormed out. I haven't seen him since and he's not returning my calls.'

'When did this happen?' Joyce was interested now.

'The day Kenneth was killed.'

'Did you tell the police about this?'

Ginger already knew the answer to Joyce's question. Nancy shook her head and avoided eye contact.

'There was no way he was involved. He liked Kenneth.'

When he was handing over cash, thought Ginger. With Nancy's level of fastidiousness, there wouldn't be any sign of Matt's fingerprints from that visit, and if he did return later, it could easily have been with a pair of gloves in his pocket.

'You need to tell the police. If nothing else, they can clear him and might even be able to get him the help he needs.'

'You're quite right, of course. It's the only thing I can do, but he's not returning my calls. Perhaps they could find him. Thank you so much; I didn't know what to do, but talking it through has really helped. I already feel a lot better.' After a moment's thought, Nancy asked, 'You will leave it to me, won't you? You won't tell the police any of this?'

Joyce started to speak, but Ginger cut her off.

'If you promise us you'll tell them, then we won't say anything.'

Nancy nodded vehemently, but once again, she looked away. Ginger wasn't going to say a word; the question was how long Joyce would wait until calling the police herself, which Ginger knew she would do. Joyce wanted to solve this mystery and a worried granny wasn't going to stop her.

'There's something I wanted to ask you, Nancy,' Joyce said. 'Kenneth had a painting by a Spanish artist that he sold recently; do you know anything about it?'

'Only that I am pleased he got rid of it. Weird, it is. There are two more and I thought it was a shame he hadn't sold them all. Trees with human limbs and strange buildings that look like fruit in deserts; they're very odd.'

Ginger could tell Joyce's cogs were turning. How far would Tobias go to get his hands on those paintings for his family's collection? And more importantly, they now had another name to add to their list of suspects: Matt.

23

Joyce sat on a large, luxurious chair as a woman painted polish on her toes. Her fingernails had already been done, the thin red-and-white stripes reminiscent of sticks of sweet rock. She had a red-and-white striped crêpe de chine skirt that she wanted to wear that evening and was having fun with the accessories.

As she enjoyed the pampering happening at her feet, Joyce was scrolling through the internet on her phone, trying to find out more about some of the names that had crossed their path so far. Right now, Matt was the strongest suspect after Tobias. She would indeed give Nancy a little time to tell the police about his argument with Kenneth, but the young man she'd seen in the photo didn't look like the kind of person capable of putting together a dramatic escape and evading the authorities for long. He was probably in a local pub, drinking cheap lager and trying to convince someone to buy him his next pint. Having said that, she wasn't going to wait for ever and would eventually call Nancy to see if she'd done anything about contacting the police.

In the meantime, she was learning more about Robert Ashmore, son of Audrey the dancer. He was easy to find as a trustee of the North Shores Dance Company; his photo and a short biography appeared on the website. It made a point of mentioning that although his role on the board was to bring financial expertise, he not only enjoyed dance from the audience, he was a keen amateur dancer himself and was a regular at the London Tango Academy's milonga, a social event involving a less-complex form of tango. These events were held twice a week and there was one this evening. Joyce loved dancing, a passion she had picked up from her mother, and her red-and-white skirt would be perfect for the occasion.

After putting her phone away, she watched Ginger enter through a door at the back of the room. She had recently managed to convince Ginger, someone who'd previously considered facials and the like a total waste of time and money, of the pleasure to be derived from spa treatments, so hadn't been entirely surprised when Ginger had announced she was going to indulge in a luxurious *Correct and Pamper* treatment. Ginger had made a few comments about the fact her face needed little correcting, which had resulted in Joyce biting the inside of her cheek so hard, she'd drawn blood. Despite Ginger having flawless skin Joyce didn't normally like to miss an opportunity to poke fun, but she didn't want to say or do anything that might put Ginger off this recently discovered appreciation of the finer things in life.

Having finished the treatment, Ginger looked as if she was glowing. She also looked a little disorientated, but she spotted Joyce and wandered over, plonking herself down in the treatment chair next to her.

'Did you enjoy that?'

'Mmmm. I think she might have drugged me, I just want to go to sleep.'

Joyce laughed. Ginger often resembled a bull in a china shop, both in size and degree of gracefulness, but she did look a little on the angelic side as she sat back into the chair with her eyes closed and a relaxed, almost dreamlike expression on her face.

'Well, you conserve your energy. You're going to need it later.'

'Why's that?'

'We are going dancing, my girl. Get those hips limbered up, we are going to burn up the dance floor.'

Ginger didn't open her eyes. 'You'd better be prepared to carry me there. Hang on, why?' The eyes snapped open. 'Why are we going dancing? I don't mind a bit of a bop, but I'm guessing you have an ulterior motive. Did you meet a man while I was in there getting my facial? Did you manage to get a date while having a manicure? I wouldn't put it past you, but why you'd want me to tag along, I have no idea.'

'Have you finished?'

'Are you going to tell me?'

'Robert Ashmore, son of Audrey. We're going to the class or club or whatever it is where he does his tango dancing.'

'And you're sure he's going to be there?'

'No idea, but there is a very good chance. It only takes place twice a week and if he's as big a fan as his bio makes out, then it's highly likely.'

Ginger groaned. 'You force me to relax, and now you suddenly want me to fly around a room performing the tango. What are you hoping to get out of him?'

'I'm wondering if he knows anything about his father having had a good reason to kill Scroop.'

'How far should we be digging around in people's backgrounds like this? He'll only tell Audrey and she seemed rather sweet. Perhaps she can tell us more if we go back.'

Joyce screwed up her face as she thought about this possible course of action.

'No, I'd like to try Robert. He'll recognise us, we can strike up a conversation and it will all look very natural. Even if he does tell Audrey, it doesn't have to look like we've been digging for information.'

Ginger sat up. 'Natural? Are you completely doolally? We arrive at their home, announce the death of Kenneth, ask questions, then suddenly appear next to him on the dancefloor, where we start up a conversation about his mother's violent ex-boyfriend. Yep, that all seems very natural to me.' She rolled her eyes and sat back again.

'You, Ginger Salt, are a woman of little faith. It's perfectly reasonable. We both love dancing; I get it from my mother, you from... well, who knows? While we are in London, we don't want to miss out on our regular dance classes, which we could always say is how you and I met in the first place. And lo and behold! We end up at the same place as him.'

'What makes you think I can dance?'

It was a fair question; they hadn't been out dancing together, but Joyce had watched her friend dance around the kitchen, or around a bar when a favourite track came on, and she'd seen Ginger grab friends in jest and twirl them. Joyce could just tell; after all, she'd spent most of her childhood and some of her teenage years around dancers. Ginger knew how to move, and Joyce was convinced that this evening she was going to show off some pretty fancy footwork.

24

---

he dance academy's milonga was held in an old but beautiful and well-maintained hall. Dark bottle-green paint covered the walls up to shoulder height, white above that. The sprung wooden floor was ideal for dancing, and at the far end, a bar glowed. It wasn't a fancy place and Ginger felt at home in its village hall-like atmosphere. When she was growing up most events, whether they be birthday parties, wedding receptions or funeral wakes, were held in either the local pub or the village hall, and Ginger was pleased that places like this still existed in the middle of London.

Half a dozen couples were already dancing as she and Joyce arrived. As they ordered their drinks and took in their surroundings, Ginger saw that dancers of all standards were welcome. That was a relief. Ginger had taken a few tango classes over the years; she loved the pure unchecked passion of the dance, but she hadn't danced in an environment like this for... oh, she couldn't remember. She was more preoccupied with the idea of seeing Joyce dance for the first time. That alone would be worth the trip; they could always run into Robert another way.

After much debate and many wardrobe changes, Joyce had

opted to wear the same red dress as the night before and Ginger agreed with that decision. Once Joyce had tied a white scarf around her waist, her nail polish didn't look quite as out of place; in her red-and-white skirt, she'd resembled a circus big top. The split in the fabric that led all the way up to Joyce's thighs was going to get a workout tonight.

Ginger wore silk trousers again: a black pair with a loose orange vest top under a sheer black shirt which she had tied at the waist. She had known that a trip to London with Joyce would involve more outfits than she could ever plan for and her new approach to packing – if it fits, chuck it in – was paying off.

They both ordered Negronis, Joyce because the colour went with her dress, Ginger because ordering the same took a lot less brain power and she had no idea what she was in the mood for. But before they could make their way to a table, Joyce was whisked off by a man who offered her his hand, which did not surprise Ginger in the slightest. She pulled up a chair at the end of one of the tables that lined the edge of the room and enjoyed the herby bitter cocktail. It had been a good choice.

The man dancing with Joyce looked as though he was a little afraid of her, another thing which made complete sense to Ginger. He held her close, but not too close, and Joyce... well, she had knees made of elastic as she kicked her heels behind her. Her hips must have had a good dose of WD40 as well because they certainly didn't move like those of a woman of Joyce's advancing years. Everyone moved at a fairly sedate pace, practising their steps, except Joyce, who didn't lack any confidence.

Ginger was eventually asked to dance by a nervous young man who led her around the dancefloor with a consideration that she wished more men his age had. *He probably thinks I'm old enough to be his grandmother*, she concluded. But then, she was.

. . .

After about twenty minutes, Joyce refused the hand of the same young man who had danced with Ginger and joined her friend. A fresh drink in her grip, she announced she wanted a break.

'It's all rather invigorating, don't you think? I had no idea how much I missed dancing.'

'Did your mother teach you?'

'Some, yes. I attended the dance classes at her school once she set that up, but I'd already learnt a lot from her and her friends from as soon as I could walk. As an adult, I attended classes from time to time, depending on which husband I was with.'

'Were any of them keen dancers?'

Joyce laughed. 'My God, no. The first marriage only lasted a couple of weeks so there wasn't time to fit in a dance class. The others – it just wasn't their thing.'

Ginger waited a moment, wondering if this was the time to ask, and then decided to go for it.

'Why was your first marriage so short?'

Joyce kept her eyes on the dancers as she replied. 'He was a bit of a cad from the off, but I was young and foolish enough to fall for his charms. I wasn't *that* foolish, however. When he spent our wedding night at the races, gambling away any money we'd been gifted on the dogs, I knew I'd made a mistake. A couple of weeks later, I packed my bags and moved back home. Mother always knew he was no good, but I'll give her her due: she warned me, but knew when to step back and let me make my own mistakes. And she never said *"I told you so"* when I arrived on her doorstep, bag in hand.'

There was nothing Ginger could say to that.

'May I?' A large man, in both height and build, offered his hand to Joyce.

'No, you may not. I told you last time.'

He smiled and walked away, looking as though he hadn't registered her gruff tone.

'What was that all about?'

'I danced with him once earlier and he was all hands, seemed to think that my backside was a shelf to rest his mitts on. Every time I corrected him, he put them right back. It was like he was testing the ripeness of a melon.'

Ginger laughed. 'I'm amazed he still has his hands attached.'

'If he doesn't give up, then I can't guarantee that he will. He's still looking over here, grinning. I give it ten minutes until he tries again.'

'Then I give it ten minutes and fifteen seconds until his death.'

'Ten minutes and ten seconds. I don't mess around.'

25

They both spotted Robert arrive at the same time. Wearing a pale-grey suit and a rather eye-catching bright-orange tie, he looked as if he had come straight from the office. As he stood at the top of the stairs that led into the hall and surveyed the mass of bodies, he smiled and seemed extremely happy to be there.

The smile slipped a little when he spotted Joyce and Ginger looking up at him. He swapped his bag from one shoulder to the other and made his way down, ordering a drink at the bar before walking straight over to them. He looked rather stern, but not angry; there was a sense of control about him, as though he knew he could handle whatever they put to him.

'I knew I'd see you two again. Didn't expect it to be here, though.'

'What made you so sure our paths would cross?' Joyce was genuinely curious.

'You appear out of nowhere, have significant information to impart to my mother, ask questions about the past. You're up to something.'

Joyce liked this man. He wasn't daft, not like most of the men she'd had dealings with. She decided that a direct approach was needed this time. No games; no pretending that their interest was entirely innocent. If he was involved, either he'd give himself away or they'd find out by another route.

'We're trying to learn more about Scroop Harrison de Clare; we think his murder might be connected to that of Kenneth Gaddy.'

'And you think Mother was involved?'

'Not in his death, no, but she might know something, remember something from back when Scroop died which could identify the killer and tell us something about the more recent events.'

'And then there's your father.' Ginger appeared to have taken her cue from Joyce and got straight to the point. 'Did he ever say anything? When he died, did you find anything out…'

'About his involvement? You think my father killed Scroop?'

'No, no.' Ginger added quickly, 'But there might have been something in his papers which would help identify the killer, or lay out what Scroop was involved in.'

'What Scroop was involved in was abusing women. He was a nasty, manipulative man. There was no doubt he was charming – even my father said as much – but he typically used those charms on younger girls.'

'How young?' asked Joyce, feeling her blood start to boil.

'No, not that young. He was very careful to remain within the law, but they were young enough to be inexperienced and have no clue when they were being taken for a ride. My mother was a very talented, excited and innocent young woman when she met Scroop. Although she is unfailingly kind, she is also highly intelligent, but from everything I've heard, I'm not surprised she fell for him. Even the men found him charming and wanted him for a friend, or more. The fact that he threw his money around probably helped, but it didn't stop him getting killed when he left one woman too many with a black eye.'

'Like your mother?' Joyce tried to soften her voice as much as possible.

'Like my mother, yes.'

'Did she ever talk about who might have killed him?'

'No, and before you ask, yes, I did wonder if my father had something to do with it. But Mother said he was away the night Scroop died. He was visiting his parents in the north of the country, so I never gave it any more thought.'

Joyce looked over at Ginger. She was draining her second glass of Negroni and the ice was rattling as she tried to extract the last few drops. She put the glass down and turned to Robert.

'And what about Kenneth? Your mother said you had a lot of dealings with him.'

'On the committee, yes. He was past his prime, couldn't contribute as much as he used to, but he was still passionate about the work of the company and he was held in enough esteem that he could extract favours and encourage donations. He brought with him connections, but they were dying away, quite literally.'

Joyce noticed her admirer hanging around. As she'd suspected, he hadn't got the hint. She tried to ignore him as she listened to Ginger and Robert.

'Had you seen him recently?'

'Not for about a month. We have a committee meeting scheduled for next week and I was expecting to see him then.' Robert took off his tie and put it in his bag before undoing the top couple of buttons on his shirt. 'And no, there was nothing unusual and he didn't seem worried about anything.'

'That's in a roomful of people,' Ginger noted. 'What about his phone call to your mother?'

Robert shot her a look that Joyce couldn't quite interpret. Surprise? Concern?

'What call?'

'Your mother said he had tried calling her and left a message on the answerphone. You didn't know?' Ginger's cogs were clearly turning. 'Did he try calling another time?' she asked.

'Tried, yes. She wasn't around when he rang.'

'But I'm guessing you were,' Ginger stated. This made Joyce sit up.

'What do you mean? My job is demanding, often has me working weekends as well as weekdays. I'd be out at work.'

'Not every day, you're not. You were home when we came around, so I guess you can work from home if you want. I'm also guessing that he called one day and you answered, then didn't tell your mum.'

Robert looked a little like a rabbit in the headlights. Ginger had struck gold and Joyce was impressed.

'How did you know?' Robert asked.

'I didn't, but I'm not stupid and decided to take a chance.'

Robert drained his glass and placed it next to Ginger's. 'Yes, Kenneth called. I thought it was something to do with the company, to discuss the last meeting, I don't know. When I told him my mum wasn't in, he started talking to me about Sheridan Knight – had he been in touch? Did I know anything about Scroop's death? Had my father said anything? Had Mum said anything? Of course, I couldn't help him. Mum hadn't said anything to me about it at all; not recently, anyway.'

'And you didn't tell her Kenneth had called and been asking these questions?'

'I didn't see what good could come from digging up the past. It wasn't a happy time in Mum's life and there is no need for her to relive it. I can protect her from that much.'

'What more did Kenneth say? Was he worried about anything in particular? Had he been threatened?' Robert was starting to tire of this, Joyce could tell, but she wanted a little bit more.

'No, nothing like that.'

'And did he – your father, I mean – ever say anything else

about Scroop? Beyond saying that he was a charming thug, that is.'

Joyce could immediately tell from the look on his face that Robert was finished with the conversation.

'Ladies, I can understand your interest. Your mother was around at the time, Joyce, and you might have unanswered questions, but I'm not interested and neither is Mum. Now, I came here to dance, so if you'll excuse me.'

'Useful?' Joyce asked when Robert had walked away.

'Perhaps. I need another drink to help get the old grey cells going. You?'

'Yes, please, that would be...oh, for heaven's sake, NO!'

26

*G*inger watched the stand-off, Joyce looking as though she wanted to rip the head off the man who had been pestering her to dance and chew on it for a while, and he was clearly incapable of reading the signals.

'Come on, we dance extremely well together,' he insisted. 'We have a connection. It'll be fun.'

Joyce said nothing.

'I was also thinking, we could enjoy a bit more dancing, then head out for something to eat. How about it?' He beamed, looking as if he had just made the most impressive offer and she was guaranteed to accept. What was it going to take for him to realise that his luck was most definitely not in tonight?

Ginger stepped forward. 'What are you doing?'

'Your friend here is a great dancer. We should be out on that dancefloor.' He looked back at Joyce. The words *'And then spend the rest of the evening together'* hung in the air.

'She's no friend of mine,' Ginger growled and registered the shock on Joyce's face. 'That's my wife and if you don't back off...' She took another step forward and placed herself between Joyce and her suitor. Joyce now looked as surprised as he did.

'Oh, I'm sorry, I'm really sorry. I would never... I do have principles... I just never saw... you're not wearing wedding rings, either of you.'

'We don't believe in symbols of possession. Now go and find someone else to harass.'

He backed away, apologised again, and then disappeared into the throng stepping and twirling around the dancefloor.

'Wow, he might be a handsy, self-obsessed Lothario, but he really does have morals,' Ginger said, genuinely surprised.

'I doubt it, I think he was just terrified of you. Who knew you could be so scarily possessive?'

'He needed to back off and it drives me nuts when someone won't take no for an answer. Come on.' She held out a hand to Joyce.

'What?'

'We need to keep up the act or he'll be back for another go.'

'You want me to dance with you?'

'Yes and I'm leading.'

'You're blooming well not.' Joyce stood with her hands on her hips. 'I'm the better, considerably more experienced dancer. *I* will be leading.'

Ginger let out a sigh of exasperation. 'Alright. This time only, though. Next time, I'm...'

Before she could finish, Joyce had grabbed her hand and pulled her out onto the dancefloor. With one hand around Ginger's waist, Joyce gave a sudden tug and jolted Ginger into position. For someone who looked as if they were as rigid as a flagpole half the time, Joyce was surprising relaxed and embraced the fun and humour of the milonga style of dance. Ginger could see that Joyce was more than a little surprised to see how fluid and easy her own movements were, too.

Ginger enjoyed the fast-paced steps and found it easy to imagine that she was in Buenos Aires; it had certainly been hot enough in London. She laughed out loud as Joyce led her quickly and effortlessly around the floor, and Joyce grinned back, looking as though she was utterly at home and having as much fun as Ginger. Mind you, Joyce wouldn't be likely to get any more offers to dance from men tonight, even charming, well-mannered types. That would probably remove the smile from her face.

Ginger opted to keep that revelation to herself and focused on what her feet were up to. This was too much fun to spoil with a sudden dose of reality.

'I didn't know I had it in me.'

Ginger laughed as she skipped along the pavement. Her feet were sore and her legs ached.

'I can't remember the last time I had so much fun, and all in the company of my wife.' She grinned at Joyce, who appeared similarly energised.

'I'll let you have fun with that for a while, but if it puts off Mr Right from making his advances, you'll be in trouble.'

'You mean I have to share you? Never! You're my one and only, and I am your one and only.'

Joyce's eyes rolled up into her head.

They had opted to leave the underground a couple of stops early and walk the final mile or two back to the flat. Their sore feet weren't going to prevent them from enjoying the summer evening. They had got off at Green Park and made their way along Pall Mall, past the Gilmore Club and towards Trafalgar Square. Once in the square, Ginger was tempted to stick her feet in one of the fountains, but she didn't think she had the energy to climb up, so she opted to lean against the edge and wave her hands through the water.

'Ginger Salt, stop it! You have no idea what's in there.'

'Rainwater? No, it's not rained for days. Well, it's still just water.'

'Someone might have peed in it.'

That gave Ginger reason to pause for a moment, but she didn't remove her hands. It was too pleasant.

'I'm not going to drink it.'

'Well, you knock yourself out, and if you're ill tomorrow, don't come running to me.' Joyce started walking away slowly and Ginger pulled her hands out of the water, placing them on her feet, which were really starting to ache now. She watched Joyce come to a sudden stop, staring at something or someone.

'What, wifey, seen someone you know?'

Joyce ignored Ginger's joke, which made her pay attention.

'Is that Tobias?' Ginger asked, catching up with her friend. Joyce nodded. Standing side by side, they watched Tobias Harrison-Hunt on the upper level of the square, beyond him the looming building of the National Gallery, a dark block surrounded by streetlights and steel-grey sky. He was talking to someone, and from his body language, Tobias was the one in charge. It seemed as if he had a lot to say. The man standing opposite him looked away from time to time, making the occasional attempt to chip in, but rarely having the opportunity. Tobias was clearly a man who liked the sound of his own voice and the other person was getting a great demonstration of this.

If he had bothered to turn around, Tobias would have spotted the two women straight away. It was obvious they were watching, and their outfits, or rather Joyce's, were hardly subtle. The younger, rather untidily dressed man didn't seem interested in being there. He made a move to leave and Tobias grabbed him by the shirt. Ginger was worried they were going to witness a fight and she didn't fancy Tobias's chances very much.

'He's familiar,' said Joyce. 'That younger man, I've seen him before.'

Ginger squinted; she knew what her friend meant. Maybe they had seen him in a bar or café, perhaps the one where they met Nancy. That was it! The café.

'It's Matt, Nancy Binns's grandson. She showed us his picture, remember?'

'Well I never,' said Joyce. 'This is extremely interesting.'

27

*A*fter watching Tobias and Matt for a while, they had realised that nothing was to be gained from hanging around and hailed a black cab to take them back to the flat. It was late; Joyce was quite the night owl, but she knew Ginger was a 'tucked up with a good book' kind of gal. Unless you cracked open a bottle of bourbon, in which case she could keep going until the early hours. The more time they spent together, Joyce had realised, the more Ginger came out of her slipper-wearing, blanket-snuggling, mystery-reading shell. It was as though Joyce was bringing back the old Ginger, or at least that was what she liked to tell herself, having never met 'the old Ginger'.

Neither of them had wanted to head straight to bed, so they had raided Jenny's collection of liquor and were now sitting out on the balcony. Ginger already knew what kind of bourbon Jenny had – after all, she had bought it especially for Ginger's visits, which were so far apart these days that she had commented on the dust that sat atop the bottle – while Joyce had whipped up a Brandy Alexander for herself. They looked out across the Thames, their feet resting on the railing of the balcony, cardigans around their shoulders.

'Was Matt selling him drugs?' Ginger asked between sips.

'Tobias doesn't look like a user, but then I suppose it could be entirely recreational or special occasions. I can't imagine he'd buy it so publicly, though. That's not it. If Tobias does have reason to want Kenneth out of the way, he's hardly likely to want to get his hands dirty; he'd have someone else do that for him. Matt has access to Kenneth's house and could probably be bribed; he was clearly short of cash.'

'How do they know each other, then?'

'No idea. Perhaps Tobias went to see Kenneth, saw Matt coming out of the house, approached him and offered him money.' It all seemed quite reasonable to Joyce. She couldn't be sure how they knew each other, but there was a wealthy man who she believed had secrets, and a young man who had problems with drugs and money. Matt would be an easy target for Tobias to manipulate, which presented Tobias with the means and opportunity, and at least two motives had come to light.

'There's someone else that we need to consider as a potential killer,' said Ginger without raising her eyes from the view, the glass of bourbon still hovering at her lips.

'Mmm?'

'Nancy. She certainly had the opportunity, and she could clean the place after she'd done it.'

'And her motive is?'

'Matt. For all we know, she's the one who was encouraging Kenneth to help her grandson. She probably knows how much money Kenneth had: that house is worth a bob or two, the antiques are valuable, she may have seen his accounts as she was cleaning his study, and yet he refused to help Matt. She might have been angry enough to kill him.'

It was a stretch, but Ginger had a point. Joyce needed to lay it all out.

'Nancy, Matt, Tobias, Robert.' Joyce went down the list of suspects. 'Nancy and Matt have motives in the here and now,

Tobias and Robert have links to Scroop, and Tobias wants Kenneth's other two Cozar paintings. It's too farfetched to think that Tobias would be trying to protect Scroop's murky reputation; that was well known and as he was murdered, it's been out in the open for decades and can't be hidden. If Kenneth wasn't willing to sell *all* his Cozar paintings and Tobias was determined to return them to the family, then there is a motive right there. But there might be something else; Tobias really wasn't happy that we were sniffing around.

'Robert, he's a possibility. After our talk with him tonight, he's not top of my list, but if his father was involved in Scroop's murder, then he has a very good reason to want to keep that secret dead and buried. He's close to his mother and doesn't want anything to upset her. If he hid a phone call from her, he'd certainly want to make sure that the knowledge her beloved husband was a killer was kept from her.'

'Audrey told him that his father was away the night Scroop died,' said Ginger.

'We have no idea if that's true as we don't know what, if any, evidence there is to prove it. Maurice could have lied to her; she could be covering for him.'

They sat in silence for a while. The temperature had dropped considerably, but it was still a nice night.

'One thing that crosses my mind...' Ginger paused, waiting for a response.

'Hmm?'

'We've rather dismissed Kenneth's concerns about Sheridan. He wasn't entirely convinced that Sheridan had been killed, but it had crossed his mind. It might be worth calling the care home he lived in and seeing if he had any visitors.'

'We'd never be able to prove anything.'

'No, but if Kenneth was onto something, that would give us another angle to look at.'

Joyce nodded; it might not be a complete waste of time.

They settled back into a comfortable silence before Ginger looked over at her. 'You know what I think?' Her voice had an air of mystery about it and Joyce knew she was about to wind her up over something, so waited in silence for her to get on with it. 'You'd make the right woman very happy. I didn't think about it until this evening, but you were totally at ease, pretending to be my wife.'

Joyce laughed. 'You didn't give me a lot of choice, although it was a brilliant distraction. And anyway, I've tried that: an illicit entanglement with Barbara who worked at a makeup counter. It was a one-night-only thing when I was in my twenties; just didn't do it for me.' Joyce laughed again as Ginger spat out a mouthful of bourbon.

'Bleedin' hell, I didn't expect that.'

'Based on the amount of drink you've just lost down your cleavage, I can tell.' They both laughed as Ginger used a cardigan sleeve to clean herself up. 'No, not my thing, but I was very honoured to be your wife for the evening,' said Joyce, before winking and taking another mouthful of her Brandy Alexander.

28

'*I*'d like to talk to someone about Sheridan Knight.'

Ginger poured them both a second cup of coffee as Joyce made the phone call to the Ash Lodge Care Home. She had slept like a log, but then she had danced like a twenty-one-year-old, and boy could she feel it. But it was a good sort of ache that had settled into her joints, the kind that told her she had worked hard and reminded her that she still had it in her, even if she had rolled out of bed with a groan rather than a skip and a jump. She was musing over whether or not to start dancing more often as she covered her toast with a thick layer of butter. Toast was, as far as Ginger was concerned, a butter delivery system. If you didn't leave teeth marks in it when you took a bite, you hadn't put enough on.

'Me? I'm… I'm his niece. No, no, I understand; I don't want to know anything that was on his records… no, I realise that. I was just trying to find out if he'd had any visitors the day that he died.'

Joyce looked over at Ginger wide-eyed; she was clearly struggling.

'Yes, of course privacy is extremely important… yes, even in death, only it's just that it would give us so much peace if we knew he wasn't alone when he… he went…'

Ginger was enjoying this. Joyce was never the type to mince words and was probably fighting the urge to say *'When he snuffed it'.*

'Well, just before he… he passed on, then. He did? Do you know who it was? It really would help us to heal. Oh, a solicitor. Medium height, grey hair, full figure. Yes, of course, that sounds just like something Uncle Sheri would do. Very organised man. Thank you so much.'

Joyce hung up.

'Uncle Sheri?'

'Well, it had to sound like we were close. I didn't think she was going to give anything away; she thought I wanted the ins and outs of his final moments. Anyway, a few hours before they found he had snuffed it…'

Ginger grinned. She'd been right.

'Snuffed it?'

'Shuffled off this mortal coil, bought the farm, gave up the ghost, whatever. When you're gone, you're gone; you're not around to hear what people are saying, so no point pussyfooting. So, a few hours before he *died…*' she gave Ginger a pointed look '…he did have a visitor: his solicitor. Apparently, Sheridan wanted to make sure everything was in order. One or two of the staff commented on his impeccable timing.'

'The solicitor's or Sheridan's?'

'Both, I imagine. He's a local solicitor, though; he's the one they bring in if a resident doesn't have anyone else they prefer to use, so it's not particularly suspicious. It's a dead end, so to speak.'

Ginger rolled her eyes as she took another bite of toast, scattering crumbs on the table as she spoke.

'So, what are our plans for today?'

'What are you, eight? Don't talk with your mouth full. You can do what you like, I'm meeting Jim. I want to find out more about the night Scroop was killed.'

'Then I will go to Hatchards. I have a hankering for some more mystery books. I've just finished one by Josephine Tey and all this investigative work has me craving more. Maybe I'll pick up some tips.'

'Yes well, you can start by getting yourself a copy of *A Modern Girl's Guide to Etiquette* and memorising its contents before you next have a meal with me.'

Ginger flicked a crumb at her across the table.

29

*J*im was as smartly dressed as ever when he greeted Joyce outside the stage door. He beamed at her as she approached.

'You really do look like your mother, a bit more colourful maybe.' He looked down at her skirt – she had finally donned the red-and-white striped crêpe de chine one, and her matching nails had made it through the previous night without a single chip. A red silk blouse, matching bag and shoes completed the outfit. 'You look like you're about to go on stage, *My Fair Lady* or somethin' like that.'

'There is no occasion that doesn't deserve a bit of colour, and a cheerful outfit makes other people smile. It's my way of giving back to the world.'

'Well, you've certainly cheered me right up. Now, I've got an hour; the lad from the post room is covering for me, but he's done that quite a lot recently and I don't want to take advantage. Come on, let's go and get a sticky bun.'

He held out his arm and Joyce looped her own through it. She wasn't usually quite so easy-going about displays of affection, but she wanted him on side. Plus it gave her some comfort, knowing that he had spent time with her mother, so she decided to relax a bit and make an old man happy.

Jim led her to a small Italian café where the staff all seemed to know him. Almost before their bottoms had hit the seats, a large sticky bun the size of a dinner plate had been placed in front of them. Joyce decided to ignore it. Jim unfolded a napkin and tucked a corner in the neck of his crisp white shirt.

'They never used to have these, but once they knew how much I like this sort of thing, they put them on the menu just for me. It's not going to help my cholesterol levels, but I only allow myself one a week.'

One a week? Once a year is too much, thought Joyce as she straightened out her skirt and made sure it flowed evenly down each side of the chair.

'It's lovely to see you again, but I'm guessing this isn't just a nice catch-up. You have something you want to talk to me about?'

'I do. I was wondering what you could remember about the night of Scroop's murder.'

If Jim was surprised, he didn't show it.

'You know, I hadn't thought about that time for ages, not until you came by. But now, well, I've been thinking about it a lot, remembering your mum, what a remarkable lady she was, and how much fun we all had back then.'

Joyce had reached into her bag as he spoke. She pulled out some of the photos she had been carrying around; she liked to look at them, particularly the one of the group of friends ready for a night out. She imagined she could hear their laughter.

The photo of Jim and the dancers was amongst the collection she spread on the table.

'Let's have a look.' Jim reached for the photo. 'My God, I look young, barely out of nappies.' He laughed at his own comment. 'I really was star-struck. Spent a lot of my time unable to speak, I was so in awe of all these women; infatuated with a lot of them 'n' all. You know when this one was taken, right?' Jim picked up Joyce's favourite photo.

'In 1953, around the time Scroop was killed.'

'This picture was taken the actual night Scroop died. I know because it was one of the girls' birthday and we were all going out after the show. I'd been invited as well and I bought that sweater especially; I wanted to make a good impression. Well, a boy can dream.' He tapped the photo of himself with the dancers, which he had replaced on the table, and grinned. 'You can't see on the photo, but it was a very smart burgundy red. I thought I was the bee's knees.

'Anyway, more importantly, that was the night that Scroop was killed. Look at him, thought he was God's gift.' Jim scrutinised the photo still in his hand. 'It was a shame, really; it was a horrible night in lots of ways, but everyone wanted to have a good time.'

'Lots of ways? So not just the murder?'

Jim sighed. 'Look at Kenneth. Does he look happy to you?'

Joyce took the photograph from Jim and examined it more closely. Jim was right; Kenneth was smiling, but it was forced, it didn't extend to his eyes. Clearly, he wasn't as relaxed as the others. Joyce had never noticed before, but now it had been pointed out to her, it was impossible to miss.

'What was wrong, do you know?'

Jim nodded. 'I know all about it. You see, in those days, folks like Kenneth... well, it just wasn't accepted. People thought they were freaks, but not in the theatre, or not so much. We've always been a very welcoming world, you see; if you're different, then you can probably find a home with us. Nowadays, you can marry who you like and people like Kenneth don't have to hide who they are.

'We all loved Kenneth, but Scroop, he liked to find people's weaknesses, and then start poking and prodding. He liked to have control. Kenneth had a young man, Henry; he was a writer and they were very much a pair. Lovely blokes, both of them. I believe they were together for a long time.'

'They were still together when Henry died a couple of years ago.'

'Good, very pleased to hear that. Well, Scroop would make the occasional snide comment. He knew that everyone was on Kenneth's side so he couldn't push it too far. Anyway, that night, Scroop walked in on Kenneth and Henry in one of the dressing rooms. They weren't doing anything other than talking and holding each other, like, and it was only for a few minutes.'

It looked as if Jim was blushing. 'They didn't know I was in there. I'd been emptying bins when they came in and I hid behind a rail full of costumes. Daft, really; I'm very glad they weren't doing anything more. Well, like I said, Scroop walked in and saw them. As they went to leave, he grabbed Kenneth and kept him back in the room, locked the door so Henry couldn't get back in. Scroop made it clear what damage he could do to Henry and Kenneth's reputations. Talked about how here in the theatre they were safe, but not outside. Told him they should be careful.'

'Did he try to blackmail him?'

'No, no point. Scroop had plenty of money. I don't even think he was going to do anything, but he wanted Kenneth to know that he had power, that he could control his life in some way. I told you he was nasty. I was so angry, but I was just a kid and I couldn't do anything. Kenneth looked so scared. He wasn't the same that night. He tried to have a good time – he was always the life and soul of the party, but he just wasn't himself. I'm so pleased he and Henry stuck together, though.'

There was a few minutes of silence as Jim started to devour his sticky bun, grinning at Joyce as he chewed.

'Delicious,' he muttered, then swallowed. 'Simple pleasures, that's what I'm about now. I've had a wonderful time all these years and I'm going to miss it – all the people, the talent, the atmosphere before each show. And I must admit, I do love meeting celebrities, and I've made that place run like clockwork. But if I'm completely honest, I'm also looking forward to slowing down a bit. I have some holidays planned, caravanning. I'd like to do one of those cruises. I had hoped that it would be with Daphne, my wife, but that wasn't to be, God rest her soul. But she wouldn't have wanted me to mope; she'd have told me to get on with livin'.

'It'll probably take me a while to get used to a new routine, but boy, I can't wait. A man of leisure, that's what I'm going to be.'

30

*G*inger was up on her feet, clapping and whooping.

'Sit down, woman!' Joyce tried to pull her back into her seat.

'You're just miffed because you weren't given the lead role,' Ginger called over the sound of applause and cheers that filled the theatre. She had always wanted to see *Wicked*, the story of the wicked witch in the *Wizard of Oz* and a smash hit in the West End, and it had been as good as she'd hoped. Ginger loved a good musical; she got wrapped up in the emotion of the music, her feet would tap, she'd sing along if she could, and on this occasion, she'd had the added bonus of teasing Joyce about being a direct descendant of the wicked witch or how they must share makeup tips.

She was pleased she had booked the tickets all those weeks ago. They needed a break from the subject of Kenneth's killer, constantly talking about it and ruminating on ideas. They'd had a number of late nights, so had permitted themselves an afternoon nap before their pre-theatre dinner to recharge their batteries, but the show had also given them a boost. It was always like this for Ginger: she would leave the theatre on a high, and it wasn't just after musicals. Shakespeare, Pinter, Churchill, Ayckbourn, old or new, it didn't matter; Ginger loved live theatre and she didn't see as much of it as she would like these days.

Ginger was still humming some of the tunes as they filed out with the crowds. She grinned at Joyce.

'Wasn't it fabulous? Come on, girl, you must have loved seeing your twin up there.'

'Oh, shut up. It was certainly an enjoyable evening.'

Ginger knew that was high praise indeed, and she had spotted Joyce singing along during a couple of the songs. She wouldn't let on; she'd wait until that information was really useful. You needed to store ammunition away from time to time.

They followed some of the crowd, crossing the road carefully, walking around cars that had made the mistake of driving past the theatre just as everyone poured out, then turned down a side street and cut down a couple of alleyways. There was no point getting on the Tube; it would be far too crowded and it wouldn't take them long to walk back to the flat.

They made their way towards the Savoy hotel, resisting the urge to pop in for a cocktail, then along the Strand and down a narrow side street, before appearing in a lane cloaked in shadows, the orange glow of the streetlamps only reaching so far and leaving patches of darkness. Ginger looped an arm through Joyce's as they stepped out onto the road.

The sound of a revving engine caused her to look down the street. As she turned her head, a scooter came straight for them at speed, its small engine straining. Ginger yelped, tugging on Joyce as she spun and lost her balance. She could feel the draught caused by the scooter and its rider on her face as they came within inches of her.

As she fell, Ginger managed to pull Joyce out of the path of the scooter, but felt her ankle go over and she tumbled to the ground. Joyce somehow maintained her balance and stayed upright, but only just. The scooter stopped briefly at the end of the street, all but the rider's outline concealed by the blackness between more lamps as he or she turned to look at the two women, then rode off. Joyce let out a string of expletives in the rider's direction before looking down at her friend.

'My God, are you alright?' She helped Ginger stand. Ginger's ankle hurt, but it wasn't broken; maybe just twisted. The palm of her hand stung where she'd scraped it as she put it out to save her fall. She peered at the graze. It was a bit bloody and probably had a bunch of gravel to be picked out, but as far as she could see, that was all.

They staggered back onto the pavement, Ginger limping and Joyce trying to support her, even though that support wasn't entirely needed, which led to a slightly bumbling spectacle. Ginger sat on a low wall and took a bottle of water and a hand-kerchief out of her bag. She poured some water onto her hand, which stung like buggery, and then dabbed at it with the hankie.

'Let me do that,' Joyce said.

'You're alright, I just wanted to clean it a little. I'll look at it properly at the flat, it's not bad.'

'Can you walk? I don't mean back to the flat, we'll get a taxi, but just in general.'

'We'll find out soon enough.'

They both stared in the direction the scooter had been ridden away.

'That wasn't an accident,' Ginger said softly.

'I know.' There was a pause as they let it sink in. 'Wait here, I'll go and flag down a taxi.'

Ginger watched Joyce walk to the main street, sticking all the while to the pavement. She desperately tried to remember every physical detail of the bike and rider, but it was largely a blank. It had all happened too quickly.

31

*B*arely a minute had passed before a black cab pulled up at the kerb and Joyce leapt out.

'Come on, Hopalong, let's get you home.'

The driver slowly pulled out, talking over his shoulder.

'There's an accident up ahead, so I can't take the usual route.'

'No rush,' called back Ginger. He turned up another side street that ran parallel with the one they had walked down, then back up onto the Strand where he took a right turn. They were heading towards St. Paul's and Joyce assumed he was going to take them over Blackfriars Bridge. The traffic was light at that time of night and they moved swiftly.

'STOP!' Ginger called out. 'Look, up there.'

The taxi driver, probably used to being shouted at to do emergency stops, slammed his brakes on at the end of a side street.

'Everything alright, luv?'

'Yes. Joyce, look up there, that scooter. That was the one that came at us, I recognise the mudguard.'

It was parked under a streetlamp, a navy-blue scooter with a white mudguard on the front wheel. It was a bit rough looking;

the owner clearly didn't take care of it. More importantly, someone who appeared to be the owner was up ahead, helmet in hand, wearing a dark, bulky motorcycle jacket.

The biker stopped under a lamp and lit a cigarette. It was Nancy's grandson, Matt. Joyce reached for the door; she wasn't going to let the little sod get away with it. Ginger grabbed her arm.

'Don't you dare! We've got enough bruises for one night. We're ready.' She called the final words to the driver and they carried on their way.

Ginger was on the sofa with her leg up, a bag of frozen peas on top of her ankle. She'd cleaned up her hand and was now keeping it cool with a glass of bourbon that contained a very large spherical ice cube.

'We should get your ankle checked out,' insisted Joyce.

'Nah, it's just very sore. I don't even think I've twisted it that badly. Although I won't say no to a few more taxis from now on.'

Joyce had poured herself a glass of wine and lowered herself carefully onto one of the futons.

'Stupid chairs, suitable for students and that's about it. Well, he wanted to get a message across and we heard it loud and clear. We're going to ignore it, of course. I'm glad you spotted the scooter, and Matt. We could have wasted time looking for a man or woman, but thanks to your eagle eyes, we know exactly who it is.'

'I knew it was a bloke. Well, I assumed.'

'Why? It could have been Nancy, or someone else paid to give us a warning.'

Ginger laughed. 'Nancy? Unlikely. I might be wrong, but I do find it much harder to imagine a woman doing such a thing. Poison is much more a woman's weapon.' Ginger grinned. 'You probably have a locked cabinet full of the stuff.'

'Absolutely, so you better start watching how you talk to me, Ms Salt. I have a very long memory.'

'And a garden big enough to bury the bodies.' Ginger swirled the ice in her glass. 'Speaking of Nancy, we've already concluded she had opportunity and motive for Kenneth's murder. If she caught Kenneth off guard at the house or while he was sleeping, she could easily have hit him.'

'Not poisoned him?' asked Joyce pointedly.

'Opportunity, remember? Motive, means and opportunity, always important in a murder investigation, and Nancy had all three. I don't know how heavy one of those awards would be, but if you get enough of a swing in, you could do a heck of a lot of damage. I guess it's just as feasible that she's now roped Matt into helping her warn us off.'

'But then, she keeps calling us, and she told us about her concerns over Matt and his possible involvement.'

'Distraction? She knows there will never be any evidence against Matt: she cleaned up thoroughly and there are no other witnesses to any of his disagreements with Kenneth. At least, I'm assuming not. Are you alright?'

Joyce felt like a rag doll that had been left on a chair by a child. Her legs stuck awkwardly out in front of her, she wasn't very comfortable leaning against the back of the futon. The striped skirt, she was sure, made her look even more toy-like.

'No, I'm not. I feel ridiculous and I know I look ridiculous.' Ginger gave her a bemused nod of agreement. 'I can't do this anymore.'

Joyce rolled over onto all fours then, unceremoniously clinging on to the back of the futon, dragged herself upright. Thank God there was no one else to watch her in such an undignified state.

'There is another alternative.' She looked at Ginger, who remained silent, clearly waiting for her to continue. 'We saw Matt with Tobias only last night. Tobias has the money to pay

Matt to do something like this. However they know each other, he must know that Matt needs cash. Tobias is bound to be used to getting his own way; people like that usually are. If he wants shot of us, then he's just going to throw cash at the problem and have us scared off.'

'That sounds more reasonable than Nancy getting her grandson involved in this way. That was starting to sound like a comedy heist film.'

'You and your heist films, but you're right. Mind you, it's still perfectly feasible. But I want to talk to Tobias. If he did pay Matt to do this, then he's going to be very surprised, and worried, that we're still sniffing around.'

'We don't have an address for him. Maybe we can get it from the club?'

'No chance, they're not going to give out the personal addresses of members. Even I couldn't charm that out of them. I reckon we can track him down via his publishers, or there'll be something online. Leave that with me.'

They took a taxi to Trafalgar Square. The National Gallery wasn't due to open for another fifteen minutes, but the tourists had started to gather outside the doors. Pavement artists were beginning their chalk drawings on the ground and a couple of police officers ambled across with cups of coffee in their hands.

The two women were heading for a building around the back of a church. Joyce had spent the morning making phone calls while Ginger hobbled around making coffee and scrambled eggs. Her ankle was sore and she would take it easy – easy by her standards, at any rate. The end results were full stomachs and an address for where Tobias would be that morning.

They let themselves into the building through a set of glass doors. Ahead of them was an open reception space; the receptionist was missing in action, so they walked straight past the desk into a small hall. A couple of people were setting up tables, a large coffee urn was being plugged in and trays of pastries were laid out. In the far corner, two men appeared to be having an argument in hushed tones; Ginger was surprised to recognise them as Tobias and Matt. They weren't happy, or Tobias wasn't. It was almost like a déjà vu of the other night.

Ginger had been able to hold Joyce back in the taxi the night before, but there was no stopping her this time. As she strode across the hall, her heels clack, clack, clacking as she went, she caused everyone to look up from their jobs. Ginger walked slowly behind; the two men weren't going anywhere, so there was no need to rush.

'You're quite right to berate him,' Joyce said fiercely to Tobias. 'He completely failed in his mission; as you can see, we are still here and we aren't going to stop until we get answers.'

The blank expressions she received in return made Ginger want to laugh out loud, but she bit her tongue. Matt had never met either of them before, so the expression on his face would have been completely justified, had Ginger not suspected he had targeted her and her friend the previous night. A few seconds passed before Tobias recalled who they were. He appeared to be trying to formulate the right response; Ginger actually felt faintly sorry for him.

'I'm sorry?' Tobias managed eventually. Matt looked around as if he was trying to plan his exit.

'You paid someone – him,' Joyce jabbed a finger in Matt's direction, which caused his eyes to pop, 'to scare us off. Well, it failed, and a few scratches are not going to stop us from finding out who killed Kenneth.'

'I have no idea what you are talking about.' Tobias looked and sounded genuine. 'When was this?'

'Last night. You must have had him follow us.'

'Look, I'm really sorry if something has happened, but truly, it's nothing to do with me and I'm certain that Matt wasn't involved.' Although his apology sounded as genuine as his confusion, he was also clearly annoyed at being spoken to this way.

'You ride a scooter.' It was a statement of fact rather than a question. Matt nodded. 'And you rode it at us last night.'

'I didn't! I don't know what you're talkin' 'bout.'

Ginger couldn't read him as well as she could Tobias, but it had been his scooter, she was sure. He'd been standing near it with a helmet in his hand. It had to be him.

'Look, clearly something has happened that was rather upsetting,' said Tobias. 'How about I buy you two ladies a coffee and we can talk about it?' It sounded rather like a command.

'That's a nice idea, thank you,' Ginger said, trying to keep the mood calm.

'What about him?' Joyce was jabbing her finger at Matt again.

'Matt has work to do, don't you, Matt? I know how to get hold of him if we need him.' Matt grunted and shuffled off towards the coffee urn. 'Come on. They do great work here, but their coffee leaves a little to be desired.'

Tobias led them to a café on the corner of Trafalgar Square and fetched them all a cup of coffee.

'How do you know Matt?' asked Ginger when he'd sat down. She'd decided to steer them away from further conflict and hopefully find out what they could in other calmer ways.

'I'm the trustee of a charity that aims to help those with a drug addiction get support and go on to find work. That's one of their drop-in centres back there. I've a particular interest in the finding work element. I met Matt at a couple of events that we held and I have been doing what I can to get him some interviews. Frustratingly, he's not turned up to any of the three that I've arranged for him. I'm trying not to give up on him, but it's not easy, I can tell you.' His words sounded positive, but there wasn't much softness in his voice.

'Is that what you were arguing about on Wednesday night?'

Tobias looked briefly confused by Ginger's question, then surprised.

'You saw us? Here in the square?'

'We did. Why were you arguing?'

'I'd arranged an interview for Matt that morning. Like I said, he didn't turn up. This was with a friend's company, so I was particularly annoyed. He'd gone out of his way to do me a favour by seeing Matt, but Matt let me down. I'd been at a private viewing at the National Gallery and I saw Matt as I left. I was utterly furious. I probably shouldn't have been so harsh, but I'd had a drink and he caught me off guard. He also asked me for money and I'm not prepared to do that. I will give him support in other ways, but not that.'

Tobias spoke like a stereotypical upper-class twit, Ginger thought, and was dressed in the 'uniform' with his open-necked shirt, expensive tailor-made navy blazer, cream slacks and brown loafers, but he was revealing a different side to himself. He wasn't posturing in front of friends and people he wanted to impress at the club; he wasn't showing off. He didn't sound very friendly, but he did seem to be trying to do some good. Even if it was simply a box-ticking exercise and not actually from a place of genuine care, then so be it. People still benefitted.

Tobias looked at them both carefully before asking, 'Why did you think I paid Matt to scare you off? I didn't, but why on earth would you think I'd do something so ridiculous? Is this something to do with Scroop?'

The two women looked at one another and came to a silent agreement. Ginger explained their theory about Tobias's desire to hide some of Scroop's more nefarious dealings and that he might have wanted to keep Kenneth quiet. She didn't say that he could have killed Kenneth, more that he was frustrated by anyone who paid more attention to his family than he was comfortable with. Ginger was convinced that Tobias would laugh at them with an evil cackle, but instead he sat quietly and listened, only a slight smirk lingering on his lips, waiting until she had completely finished.

'So, I could say that's all utterly ridiculous, but as I'm a descendant of Scroop, it's not beyond the realms of possibility. Not that he did anything nefarious, I hasten to add, and nor would I. No, I did not kill Kenneth, nor did I pay Matt to silence you.

'Am I worried about my family's reputation? Yes, of course, and I have been planning a book about Scroop, but I'm not going to be moving ahead with it. Scroop did a great deal of good, particularly within the theatre world, something he was extremely passionate about. Sadly, all that good has been hidden behind his greed and his acts of cruelty. I felt that he would make an interesting focus for a book and I wouldn't shy away from what he had done, or from the way he died, but I also wanted to talk about the role he played in the history of London theatre. He was a fascinating, clever, but also extremely flawed man. Only I'm finding that most people don't want to talk to me about him, and those who do don't have a good word to say about him.' Tobias sounded so formal about the whole thing, it was hard to believe he was talking about his own flesh and blood.

'When did you decide to give up on the book?' asked Joyce, sounding unconvinced.

'The last week or so. I have a meeting with my editor next week to discuss some alternative ideas for a book. You can talk to her if you like, she'll support what I'm saying.'

'This doesn't mean that you're not unhappy at people sniffing around his truly awful behaviour. No one likes other people going through their family's dirty laundry.' Joyce had a point.

'I agree, but I'm hardly going to be worried about a couple of old... I mean, a couple of mature... two people unrelated to the police or any other official organisation asking questions. I don't think there's a great deal of harm you can do.'

Ginger still didn't like him, but she appreciated his directness, so she was simply amused by his gaffes. She sensed that Joyce agreed with her, but was less likely to see the funny side.

'You were rather cagey at the club,' Ginger said. 'What else aren't you telling us?'

He laughed, his arrogance shining through again. 'Ladies,

please. A couple of strangers start questioning me about a member of my family, and in a place that I go to relax, to be amongst peers. I'm hardly going to treat it like a therapy session and start pouring forth with all my family history, especially the skeletons in the cupboards. Anyone would be concerned and unlikely to say very much. Don't you think?'

He clearly wasn't expecting an answer. 'Look, I don't mean to be rude, but I do need to go. I hope I've helped clarify a few things for you. Here's my card, you can call me directly if you have any questions. No need to pussyfoot around. And about Matt: I don't know if he was on that scooter last night, but he is trying to get help. I'll admit not very successfully right now, but he is talking to people and the help is there when he's ready.'

'Overconfident plonker with too much money and an inflated ego,' Joyce declared as they watched Tobias walk off.

'At least his money and time are going to help a charity.'

'Only because it's what's expected of him, he does it to improve his image and fit in. I imagine everyone at the Gilmore is a trustee of some sort and donates to charity, and casually slips it into every conversation while simultaneously decrying the idea that they do it for the thanks or recognition.'

'You are feeling cynical today, aren't you. You do work for one of those wealthy plonkers.'

Joyce turned quickly to face Ginger. 'The Duke is not a wealthy plonker. Well, he is wealthy, extraordinarily so, but he's done a lot of good work and he genuinely cares. Although he does dress like everyone else in his role. I'd love to…'

'Add some colour to his wardrobe?'

'Yes, how did you…'

'Call it a good guess.'

There was a break in the conversation while they both thought about Tobias. It was Ginger who spoke first.

'We didn't ask him about the paintings.'

'I know. He'd have laughed at us.'

'True.' *Why can't people just confess to murder when pressed by a couple of old... more mature women?* Ginger wondered. 'Do you think he did it? Killed Kenneth, I mean.'

'If we were just talking about protecting his family's reputation, then I'd say no. But the paintings present a real possibility and increase the odds.'

'So what's next?'

Joyce's phone buzzed as though responding to Ginger's question. 'What does she want now?' Joyce looked at her phone as it vibrated in her hand. 'Hello, Nancy, is everything alright?'

'We need to talk to her,' mouthed Ginger.

'Alright, we'll head over. No, don't worry, I'd rather get it in person. Make sure it doesn't go missing. Yes, see you soon.' She hung up and turned to Ginger. 'Nancy has found an envelope addressed to me, she thinks it's more photos of my mum. I've said we'll collect them – you didn't have any plans, did you? Seeing a load of old rocks at the British Museum – stolen rocks at that – or the work of some obscure photographer that no one has heard of in an odd little gallery down an alleyway?'

'Philistine,' declared Ginger as she stood up. 'Some of those rocks are younger than you.'

33

It was stuffy on the Tube and Joyce was glad to be back out in the fresh air. Kenneth's street was as quiet and pretty as ever; there was no indication that someone had been horribly murdered less than a week ago. It made her wonder what went on behind some of the other front doors.

'Wouldn't someone have seen the killer come and go?' asked Ginger. She was right. They were standing outside Kenneth's house and, whether it was through the front door or from the side of the house, the murderer had to have come out onto the street or climbed over a fence at the back. Joyce thought about it for a moment, then realised what had probably happened.

'It was a very warm night. Most people would have been in their back gardens, having a barbecue. None of these gardens out front are bigger than a postage stamp and it's clear no one uses them for anything other than a minute amount of gardening. Well, those who can be bothered. You couldn't fit a deckchair out front even if you wanted to, so it's unlikely there was anyone to see them come and go.'

'Real shame, isn't it?'

The two women turned towards the speaker, an oldish man with a black Labrador on the end of a lead.

'You heard about him, the chap that lived here? He was murdered! You just don't think something like that would happen around here. Mind you, at least he was happy on his last night.'

The dog was looking up at them, as if he was waiting to hear their response. He had a grey muzzle that matched the man's own closely trimmed beard, and he seemed to have a similar expression.

'What do you mean, he was happy? Do you mean Kenneth?'

'I do. I saw in the papers that he'd been killed and I recognised him from the photograph, although I'd seen him a few times when I was out walking Bryan.' Joyce really wanted to tell him how ridiculous a name that was for a dog. 'I realised straight away that I'd seen him the evening he'd died. Bryan was having a sniff around the gatepost, so I stopped. He's old, you see, and I want him to get as much pleasure as possible out of our walks.

'Well, that man, Kenneth, he was in the window, or near the window. He was close enough to see, anyway. He was with another man and they were laughing; one of them must have said something very funny because I could hear them. That top window was open.'

Joyce and Ginger looked over at the window. It was a large bay with a row of smaller windows above, and it was possible to see a lot of the room beyond. It was entirely reasonable that two men standing fairly close to the glass would have been easy to see.

'Can you describe the other man?' Ginger asked.

'Hmm, medium height, medium build. He had on dark trousers and a white shirt. He wasn't wearing a tie, but I remember thinking that he looked like he'd come straight from work, even though it was a Sunday. He wasn't fat, but he was a bit overweight, had a belly. Wasn't unhealthy, but probably liked a pint or two, although it looked like they were drinking martinis. I recognised that funny shaped glass they come in.' The man rubbed his chin as he thought. 'He didn't have a beard, that I do remember. I always clock beards because I have one. That's about it, really. He was very ordinary, the kind of person that blends into the background.'

'Was he young? Old?' Ginger prompted.

'Oh, definitely not young, but old? Well, he might have been. Possibly. He had quite an upright bearing, good posture.'

Joyce's excitement at meeting a witness was being slowly deflated by his wishy-washy descriptions. They had as much as they were going to get from him, so she was keen to get rid of him.

'Well, thank you very much.'

'Quite alright. How come you're so curious about what he looked like? You with the police?'

'Heavens, no.' Ginger laughed, but Joyce could tell her amusement was fake. 'Just curious; can't help but be interested when something like this happens. Like you say, it's the last thing you expect in an area like this.'

'Very true, that is. Well… oh, it looks like you're wanted.' Nancy was in the window, giving them a wave. 'I better be off, Bryan needs to do another mile yet.'

They both smiled at him and he set off. Bryan didn't seem as keen to keep moving as his owner.

'Come in, come in,' Nancy called from the now open front door. 'Lovely to see you both. Excuse the boxes. Kenneth left all his books to the Theatre Museum and I decided I should make a start packing them up. It keeps me busy and if I'm not busy, I just think about what happened, and then I become a useless lump and that's no good to anyone.'

34

*N*ancy looked as though little had changed in her life, which in some respects was true, thought Ginger. She was still working for Kenneth in a way, keeping the house in order until his estate was dealt with. Ginger wondered if she still talked to Kenneth out loud.

'Come in, come in, I put the kettle on when I first spotted you outside. Make yourselves at home. Joyce, the envelope is on the dining table; I thought it might be better to sit in there.'

As they went through to the dining room, Ginger half expected Kenneth to be in the sitting room waiting for them, making martinis and readying himself to reminisce about his time with Margaret. As she passed the door, she could see that the sofa was missing, leaving a big open space. Ginger didn't want to think about why it was no longer there. Seeing all the photographs on the wall was challenging enough, their energetic young subjects beaming down at her as they were about to go on stage or enjoying celebratory drinks. There was something almost mocking about them now.

In the dining room, Joyce had taken a seat and was opening the envelope. Ginger clocked that it looked as if it had already been opened once before. Joyce pulled out a handful of black-and-white photos and they both took a cursory glance; the photos looked like more of the kind they had been poring over for the last few days. They were quickly returned to the envelope.

'Here we are. It's a bit hot for tea, but we're British so drink tea we must, especially at a time like this.'

Ginger was grateful to see glasses of water on the tray Nancy was bringing through the door; she'd drunk so much coffee that morning, she was starting to feel a bit queasy. It didn't help that the room smelt so strongly of furniture polish; Nancy clearly wasn't slowing down, even when there was no one to make a mess or kick up dust.

'He'd already separated those photos out before he died, so I knew Kenneth would have wanted you to have them.'

'Are you going to have to deal with the house and its contents?' Ginger asked.

'Yes, but not on my own. Apparently there is a cousin, quite elderly, but her daughter is going to give me a hand, once we know what Kenneth's wishes are. That's currently in the hands of the solicitors.'

They exchanged small talk for a while, Nancy telling them that once everything had been dealt with at the house, she was going to retire. She wasn't interested in working for anyone else, and Kenneth had already told her she would be left with enough money that she wouldn't need to work.

It didn't take long for the conversation to dry up and Ginger saw an opportunity.

'Matt rides a scooter, doesn't he?'

'He does indeed. His grandfather bought it for him; his maternal grandfather. My Reg died a few years back now. It was so he could get to interviews, and then eventually travel to a job easier. Apparently, they're marvellous in London, you can zip around, although you wouldn't catch me on one. I'd be terrified. It seems too dangerous to me, but he's a sensible lad. He has a helmet and he always wears a good jacket, not like some of these folks you see riding in a t-shirt. Matt had a friend who died in a motorbike accident; it wasn't enough to put him off, but it was enough to make him take precautions. He's a very safe rider.'

Joyce pulled a face at Ginger over her mug. It seemed Matt was all about safety, until he was running over old ladies.

'He's had real difficulty finding work, but I'm sure that will change. Once people get to know him, they realise he's worth them taking a chance on. He's a good kid.'

And always will be in your mind, thought Ginger. If she'd known about it, Nancy would probably claim that him riding within an inch of them was an accident, he stopped for a moment before riding off to assess the situation, and then went to get help, which arrived after they had left in the taxi.

'I'm sorry to mention it, but I assume you haven't spoken to the police about Matt and your concerns?' Joyce asked. Nancy looked down at her hands and stared into her tea.

'No, no, I want to talk to Matt. I think maybe I was being a bit silly, jumping to conclusions. He wouldn't hurt anyone and I can't do that to him. You won't tell them what I said, will you?'

This was all a bit much. Ginger didn't want to get involved in another family's drama, but they were talking about murder.

'Talk to him soon,' Joyce said firmly, 'if only to put your mind at rest.'

'Oh, I will, I will. You know, he used to talk about being a mechanic…'

As Nancy rambled on about all of Matt's skills and how well he'd done at school, Ginger's mind latched on to something the woman had said earlier. Nancy might have had another reason to get rid of Kenneth. If she had always known that she was in line for a decent financial windfall after his death, which would give her enough money to help Matt *and* enjoy her retirement, then… maybe it *was* Nancy who had set Matt on them. Ginger couldn't recall telling Nancy where they were staying, but it was possible either she or Joyce had. She had reached the point in life where she entered rooms with no recollection why, so she could have told Nancy all sorts of things, or Nancy might have overheard them talking to Kenneth the previous Saturday. Then all Matt needed to do was follow them to the theatre and be ready when the show finished.

However it had happened, it would have been easy enough to arrange. It was possible that Nancy wanted them to stop asking questions, especially if the police had dismissed Kenneth's murder as being the result of a break-in, which Nancy could have easily staged. She was a small woman, but it wouldn't have taken much strength to kill Kenneth, and Nancy's arms were likely to be toned from all the dusting she did. Or maybe she'd got Matt to do that as well.

'Ginger? Ginger!' It took her a moment to realise that Joyce was trying to get her attention. 'I'm sorry, am I interrupting your daydreaming?'

'What? No, what is it?'

'Come on, it's time to go. We should leave Nancy to her work and we have somewhere to be.'

Did they? Ginger couldn't remember. All the alcohol was destroying her brain cells; maybe it was time to cut back on the drinking. Ginger quickly dismissed that idea as the daftest thing she'd thought in a long time.

Back out on the street, the two women looked up at the house.

'Are you thinking what I'm thinking?'

Ginger looked over at Joyce. 'Possibly. Are you thinking about a hard-working housekeeper who felt that it was time she got the financial package that was coming to her?'

'I am.'

'Then you're thinking *exactly* the same as me.'

35

Joyce and Ginger went from catching up with one strong-willed woman to another. Audrey had phoned, asking Joyce if there was any way she could come and visit. Robert was at the office all day and she had something she needed to talk to her about. It had simply been the wrong time when Joyce and Ginger had dropped round earlier in the week and, of course, Audrey had been unprepared for their visit.

A taxi, train and another taxi later, they were sitting once again in Audrey's garden. A line of photos had been spread out on the table and Audrey had been looking at them as they arrived.

'The hat was a devil to keep on,' Audrey explained as they admired a tuxedo-style costume. High-cut black leotards showed every inch of the dancers' long, toned legs. 'You can't tell on these photos, but the lapels of the jackets were gold and the bowties matched. Can you believe, some men complained because it wasn't a very revealing outfit? Look, there's Margaret.'

On the back row, the striking figure of Margaret Brocklehurst had a presence which outshone all the other women. It wasn't because of her beauty, although she was extremely beautiful, but her clear strength of character. Joyce felt as if she was looking into a mirror.

Without looking up, she asked Audrey, 'What did you need to tell me?'

'I've given this a great deal of thought. I'm still not convinced you really need to know, but you seemed determined to find out more about Scroop, and Robert told me you talked to him at the milonga, so perhaps this is important.'

Joyce put the photograph down.

'You already know that your mother was a strong, beautiful woman. The girls looked up to her and many of the men fell in love with her. A few women too. But there was a kind of wall around her; she rarely allowed people to get close. I imagine that came in useful when she was raising you and your sister on her own.

'For some men, that was a challenge and she spent a lot of time fighting off over-keen suitors. To an extent, it came with the job; we all had admirers waiting at the stage door. Some even went as far as travelling the country to see us perform at another theatre, and some dancers met their future husbands that way. Things were much more innocent then than now. None of us knew the words stalker or harassment, although in hindsight, that's what it was sometimes. On occasion, a male friend might be sent to have a word if someone wasn't getting the message and that usually worked, but there wasn't the kind of trouble you hear about now. Well, maybe there was; we just didn't talk about it.

'Anyway, I told you that Margaret always looked out for the other girls, but we never really considered who looked out for her. We were young and selfish and just didn't give it any thought; we imagined she could handle herself.'

Joyce was starting to get nervous about where this was going, what Audrey would reveal about her mother, but she remained quiet, letting the woman tell her story.

'Scroop paid your mother quite a lot of attention. Even when he was dating other women, it was clear that he would have left them – including me – in a heartbeat had she returned any of the attention. Of course, your mother knew better than to get involved, and anyway, she intensely disliked him. For a time, that was that.

'I eventually confided in your mother and told her that Scroop was… well, he wasn't being very nice to me, but I'm sure she already knew. The lies I told to explain away the bruises weren't fooling anyone. I claimed that I was to blame, that I was too weak and it was my own fault for not being able to stand up to him, but your mother knew what to say to build me back up. She told me in no uncertain terms that that was rubbish.

'Anyway, not long after Scroop died, Margaret told me that he had indeed tried to take things a lot further than she was happy with. He had cornered her and she had been unable to fight back.' Audrey quickly held up a hand. 'No, he didn't do what you're thinking, but he would have done if they hadn't been disturbed. Your mother was convinced that's the only reason she was saved.'

Joyce's shoulders, which had been getting more tense and raised by the moment, dropped a little.

'Did this happen the night Scroop died?' she asked, and Audrey nodded.

'They were disturbed by a young woman, and this is why I'm telling you this in case it's important. I can't remember her name. I have tried and I have gone through all the photographs I have. I know she wasn't a dancer, but she had been backstage more than once; I think she knew Kenneth. Was it Kenneth? If so, she is the only link I can think of between Kenneth and Scroop, other than the contact they had with us through the group. I wonder if your mother had photographs that might show who she was, or even some in Kenneth's collection.'

Joyce reached for her bag. She still had with her the envelope that Nancy had given her, so she pulled out the photographs. Together, she and Audrey went through them. There were twelve or so, small and large.

Audrey smiled as she looked at them. 'We had such a wonderful time, there are so many happy memories.' But there was nothing, no one who Audrey recognised as fitting her description of Margaret's young saviour.

Ginger reached for the photos and looked at them. As Joyce and Audrey continued to talk, they were interrupted by a slight tearing noise.

'What are you doing?' exclaimed Joyce. Ginger appeared to be tearing a photograph in two and Joyce was horrified at the thought of the damage being inflicted.

'There are a couple stuck together. It looks like orange juice or something like that. See the sticky stain?' Ginger held the photo up a little higher so that Joyce and Audrey could see what she was doing. Two photographs were indeed stuck together. Ginger carefully pulled them apart, but was unable to avoid losing some of the image where they had been most firmly stuck.

She passed the freed photograph to Audrey, who gave a wide-eyed smile.

'That's her, I swear it is. I know more than sixty years have gone by, but I'd know that face anywhere. I always wanted to thank her for what she'd done for Margaret, but we never saw her again.'

Joyce took the picture out of her hands and Ginger leaned over so she could examine it too. A young woman was standing shyly by the side of four dancers. None of the dancers were familiar to Joyce and her mother didn't appear in the photograph; the young woman, however, was very familiar.

Joyce and Ginger glanced at each other, trying to remain calm and composed. After they had got over the surprise, Joyce was the first to speak.

'Well, now we know where Kenneth met his future housekeeper.'

36

'*B*loody Nora, I need a drink after that. Glass of wine?' Ginger bustled into the kitchen while Joyce took a seat at the dining table and pulled the photos out of the bag.

'If that glass of wine is actually the bottle of wine with the neck sawn off, yes. What I'm still not clear on,' Joyce shouted through the kitchen door, 'is whether Kenneth's death really is connected with the past. I doubt it's Tobias and he's the only one who might have been worried about his family's reputation. I'm not convinced that it's Robert, and anyway, that's all a bit tenuous. If these men, or rather their families weren't involved in an actual recorded crime, then they don't have anything to worry about. Everything else is just gossip and why kill someone over that...'

'OH, DRAT!'

'What?' Joyce looked up as Ginger stomped back in the room.

'We forgot to pick up anything to drink. All we've got is this cardbordeaux.' She waved a box of wine in the air. 'And I reckon Jenny opened it a long time ago.'

'Doesn't the shop downstairs have any?' There was a little

corner shop on the ground floor of the building, and Ginger recalled that it was a bit of an Aladdin's cave, so they might be in luck.

'Ooh, good idea. Back in a minute.'

Ginger returned with a bottle of white wine. 'This was all they had, but it's better than a kick in the teeth. We can make a start on this, and then increase the quality when we go out for dinner. They also had these…' She pulled out an enormous bag of puff-wheat cheesy snacks. They were actually closer to cardboard than anything that could be called food, but she needed to line her stomach.

Joyce pulled a face. 'They're all yours. Have a look at these; I've had a quick scan through as many of the photos in the box that Kenneth gave me as possible – other than the one with Scroop in and the others that we've already been examining, that is – and I've found two with Nancy in them. She's in the background, but it's clearly her.' They stared at the pictures of Nancy as though through sheer force of will, they could make the images talk and tell them what was going on. 'If she had something to hide, though, do you not think she would have removed the photo of her that was in the envelope?'

'The envelope *was* already opened. If she did have a look – and yes, I agree she would have wanted to check before giving it to you – then she wouldn't have seen it. It was so firmly stuck to the back of the other one, even you and Audrey missed it at first. Because Kenneth put that box together for you and handed it over before he died, she didn't have a chance to check the contents of that.'

'But she had years to look through Kenneth's photos,' Joyce argued. 'Why didn't she remove any with her image in every time she found one?'

'Because she didn't need to,' conceded Ginger. 'It could be

sheer coincidence – she and Kenneth met many years ago, then they ran into each other much later when Kenneth was looking to hire a housekeeper.'

'Kenneth's housekeeper who years ago just happened to witness Scroop trying to overpower a woman, and on the way to succeeding.'

We seem to have swapped the roles of Nancy's supporter and accuser, thought Ginger.

'Do you think she might have killed Scroop?' she asked.

In response to Ginger's question, Joyce held a photo up. 'Look at her. She was a waif back then; she wouldn't have stood a chance. But she must have really given Scroop a shock, otherwise he might have been able to overpower her as well. I doubt she could have done much, although Mum probably could once she had an ally.'

Ginger poured them both a glass of wine, and then thumped the cork back into the neck of the bottle. 'Nancy might have told Kenneth, though. He was a close friend of your mother's and Audrey thought he knew Nancy to some degree. Perhaps that was why Scroop was so keen to get some power over Kenneth – remember Jim told you it was Kenneth that Scroop threatened rather than Henry? Perhaps it was Kenneth who killed Scroop – the threat to his good friend *and* his partner in one night caused him to snap, even if murder wasn't his intention. Which could mean that there is still someone out there who wanted to avenge Scroop's death.'

'No, there isn't anyone else, not that we've come across.' Joyce screwed up her face after taking a sip of the wine. 'This is not going to help me think. If anything, it's going to shut down some brain cells.'

'Then you'd better go easy, you don't have that many left to begin with.'

Joyce gave a low, slow growl, but remained with the subject at hand. 'There's someone we haven't spoken to yet.' Ginger tilted her head, resembling a curious dog. 'Matt. We need to get a feel for whether or not he's telling the truth, and if he is, then we can see if there is anything else he knows. Heaven knows how we'll track him down, though.'

'Nancy can tell us.'

'No, I want to wait a while before I talk to her again. I need more time to piece this together. She's hidden her early connection to Kenneth from us this far and I'd rather we had a solid idea of any link she has to all of this before we approach her again.'

'And we need to know who the man seen enjoying a drink with Kenneth the day he died was.'

'Men in suits,' Joyce sighed, 'and boring suits at that.'

'Absolutely.' Ginger's agreement was tinged with sarcasm. 'A killer with a colourful wardrobe, that's what we're missing.'

37

*I*t hadn't been particularly hard for them to discover when and where they could find Matt. A quick call to Tobias had told them that he would be at the Trafalgar Square drop-in that evening; or at least, that was where he would typically be found. They had walked into the hall, seen that he wasn't there, and then made themselves comfortable on a bench opposite the doors.

'You know, Matt does seem to have his head screwed on in some ways,' Ginger said.

'What makes you say that?'

'Well, I know he's let Tobias down a couple of times, and he's been scrounging money off Kenneth, but at least he's coming here to get help and advice. He's not completely given up on improving his circumstances.'

'I'm not sure that trying to mow down two women on a darkened street is what I'd call having your head screwed on.' Joyce couldn't understand why Ginger was feeling so charitable towards Matt. If she hadn't been so surprised and Ginger hadn't been clinging on to her arm as she plummeted to the ground, Joyce would have gone after him, swinging her Burberry handbag around in the air and getting ready to batter him with it. The helmet wouldn't have been able to offer him much protection from her fury.

'Maybe he was desperate; maybe he hadn't intended to do any harm and was just going to scare us, which is what happened. My ankle's fine and I only have a couple of scratches.'

'You know what your problem is, Ginger Salt? You're too bloody soft. Feel this.' She handed her bag across to Ginger, who immediately dropped it to the ground.

'What the bleedin' hell have you got in that?'

Joyce reached into the bag and pulled out a very large hardback edition of *The Complete Works of Shakespeare*.

'If anyone tries it on, I'll whack them with my bag, and they'll be out for the count. Typically, Shakespeare sends me to sleep, but now he can help send someone else nighty-night in a slightly more practical fashion. It's the only thing his plays are good for.'

Ginger shook her head. 'You're doolally. You'll do your back in, lugging that around, before you even get the chance to take a swing at some poor sod.'

It was quite heavy. Joyce admitted as much, but only to herself.

'There he is!' Ginger exclaimed as Joyce returned the book to the bottom of her bag, trying not to chip a nail in the process. She watched as a tall, slim, slightly gangly lad walked, or rather lolloped, towards the doors of the hall. Joyce was surprised he didn't look scruffy or unkempt this evening. He was rather smartly dressed, actually. She chided herself for making assumptions about him, and then told herself not to get too soft. They hadn't spoken to him yet, and she wasn't going to forgive him for the scooter incident in a hurry.

'Hang on.' Ginger was already striding after Matt and caught up with him before he got through the doors. 'Matt? It is Matt, isn't it?'

He turned to face Ginger, and then stared at Joyce as she caught them up.

'Yeah.' Recognition dawned on his face. 'I don't know who you two are, but you're bonkers...' He made for the door again, but Joyce laid an uncharacteristically gentle hand on his arm.

'This is Ginger and I'm Joyce.' She had decided to take the matey approach. 'Matt, we're sorry if we gave you the wrong impression this morning. Could we take you for a beer to apologise, maybe grab a bite to eat?'

Matt looked back and forth, clearly not quite sure how to react to these two rather mismatched women.

'Alright. You're buying, though.'

'Of course.' Ginger grinned. 'Come on, let's go and get a drink.' Joyce followed on behind as Matt and Ginger held an awkward conversation while they made their way up to The Chandos, a pub of dark wood and leather seats. There was nothing fancy about it, but it had a homely feel and looked as though it would serve a decent pint. Joyce found a table in the corner while Matt and Ginger went to the bar. Ginger was far too relaxed for Joyce's liking; she really hoped her friend was being careful about what she said.

On their return, Ginger placed a glass of white wine in front of her. Joyce took the opportunity to have another look at Matt. He wore a navy blue polo shirt, jeans and clean white trainers. He needed a shave, but his blonde stubble was barely noticeable; only if you looked closely could you tell.

Matt spotted that she was giving him the once-over and locked eyes with her in a challenge. *Cocky sod*, she thought.

'Pinot Grigio, I assumed that'd do,' announced Ginger. 'Right, so Matt knows the score.'

'The score?' Joyce enquired, pulling her eyes from his to stare at Ginger.

'I'm not stupid,' he said after taking a big gulp of Guinness.

'No one goes from spitting fire and accusations in the morning to taking you for a pint in the pub of your choosing and paying for food in the evening. Not when that drop-in place has free refreshments. What is it you want to know about Kenneth that my nan can't tell you?'

Joyce had given Ginger a sharp kick under the table as Matt was speaking, and was now glaring at her. This was not the plan. They hadn't actually had a plan, but even so, this was definitely not it. Ginger just shrugged and didn't flinch, and Joyce wondered if she'd actually kicked the table leg instead.

'How mad at Kenneth were you for not giving you any money the last time you asked?' Joyce decided she might as well get stuck in. Matt rolled his eyes.

'Give me a break, you think I'd kill him over that? I soon moved on.'

'You didn't think about it for a few hours and get more and more angry?' Joyce suggested.

'No, of course not. He's helped me out a lot over the years and he's always been good to my nan.' His voice sounded appropriately hurt by the suggestion, but there was a hard look in his eyes which made Joyce feel uncomfortable.

'Did you go back to see him again on the day he died?' Ginger kept her voice soft. Matt shrugged.

'Maybe, I don't keep a diary. I don't know.'

'The police would have asked the same question and I'm guessing they insisted on you working it out, so did you?' Joyce asked.

'What is this, bad cop, good cop?' He gave a cockeyed smile. 'Yes, I went back round. He wasn't there.'

'But you can let yourself in, can't you? You've got a key?' It was more of a question from Ginger than an accusation.

'I used to. He took it off me, wouldn't give it back until I was clean – you know, totally off drugs. So no, I couldn't get in.'

'But surely your nan would have told you where Kenneth hid a spare key, under a plant pot or something. Or you could just break in.'

Ginger gave her a dig under the table. Joyce couldn't help it, she didn't like him. There was something about Matt that got her back up. He was far too full of himself, that was it.

'What time of day did you go round?' Ginger asked. 'The second time, I mean. It would be helpful to know.'

'About four. He wasn't in, so I left.'

'Why did you want to see him?'

Matt shrugged again. 'It didn't feel right, leaving it the way we had earlier. I just wanted to talk.'

Joyce wasn't convinced they were going to get a different story out of him, but she still wasn't sure about him. Often when she and Ginger tried to get information out of people, she'd get a feel for them, and Matt unsettled her. He seemed in charge of the conversation, not them.

A member of bar staff walked over and put a giant serving of pie and chips in front of Matt. He gave a nod of thanks in Ginger's direction and started eating.

'One more thing before we leave you to eat,' said Joyce. 'Why did you try to run us over last night if you don't have anything to hide?'

He paused, but didn't look up at her. Instead, he stabbed a chunk of pastry with his fork and allowed a small smile to cross his lips.

'Why would I want to run you over?' It sounded like a genuine question.

'You tell me. You ride a scooter, a blue one with a white mudguard, don't you?' He nodded. 'So why did you do it? Or should I say, who paid you to scare us off?'

He slowly looked up at Joyce, locking eyes with her again. 'I didn't try to knock anyone over.'

Joyce stared back at him. The bravado wasn't doing a good

job of hiding what sounded like genuine surprise and hurt. She believed him. London was a big city with a lot of scooters. Okay, the paint job on the scooter that was ridden at them was distinctive, but maybe not that unusual. Perhaps they'd been barking up the wrong tree.

38

*I*t was their last full day in the city and Ginger had rather hoped that she could squeeze in a couple of the galleries that had been on her list, but remained neglected as they tried to work out who had killed Kenneth. But despite her craving to see an exhibition on Turner at the National Gallery, she knew that she wouldn't be able to enjoy it with the mystery surrounding Scroop and Kenneth still swirling around her head.

She had made coffee and sat out on the balcony, trying to distract herself by identifying as many of the buildings over the river as possible. Skyscrapers like the Gherkin, the Walkie-Talkie or the Strata, which resembled an electric razor, were of no interest to her and if anything made her rather depressed. It was buildings like Somerset House or the Inns of Court, where it was easy to imagine hundreds of years of history still inhabiting the brickwork and the grounds, that fascinated her. She loved the smaller churches, St. Bride's with its wedding-cake spire, or St. Etheldreda's that dated back to the reign of Edward I. Those were the buildings that impressed her; they didn't have to scream that they were the newest, tallest or most expensive. They didn't have penthouse apartments or gyms and swimming pools. Their mere existence carried out the weighty task of holding on to history, and Ginger quietly thanked them for that.

'Good morning,' trilled Joyce as she strode onto the balcony. Ginger's moment of contemplation was firmly over. 'I just don't understand that lot. I'm not convinced that we're meant to begin our days with such unnecessary physical exertion, especially on a Saturday. Weekends are for rest and relaxation.' She was leaning over the balcony and watching the joggers who ran along the path below. 'Start slowly, wake the body carefully. No shocks to the system.'

'Thank you, Dr Brocklehurst. Now sit down and start the day without any unnecessary exertion of your tongue.'

Joyce stuck said tongue out at Ginger and plonked herself down into a chair. She closed her eyes, took a deep breath in and a longer one out with an exaggerated 'aaaaaahhhh'. Then she turned and faced Ginger.

'Now then, I've been thinking…'

'Well, that didn't last long. Five seconds of peace, is that all you can manage?'

'I've a lot on my mind.'

'Of course you have. It must take a lot of hard work and deliberation to match your shoes with your nail polish.'

'If it wasn't for the fact that you have volunteered to make breakfast, I'd give you a piece of my mind.'

'I haven't volunteered to… oh, you should be so lucky.' Joyce kept her stare steady. 'Oh alright, but not right now. I'm still drinking my coffee and until you rolled onto the balcony, I was enjoying the calm of the morning.'

'We don't have time for your morning meditations. We need to think. We leave tomorrow and we still haven't figured this out, and there's no need to tell me that it's the job of the police. I know we can find the answer. It's out there, we just haven't put the pieces together yet.'

Ginger sighed. 'I won't be telling you anything, I happen to agree. I didn't get much sleep last night because I was trying to piece it all together.'

Ginger put her head back and closed her eyes as Joyce continued to talk.

'I'll be honest, I'm ruling out Tobias. He might have wanted to return his family's collection of José Antonio Cozar's paintings, but I don't think he would have told us about his interest if he had just killed Kenneth for that reason. Besides which, he was much younger than Kenneth; he could have just waited until the old man died of natural causes, and then bought them from whoever inherited them.'

'If he's a man used to getting what he wants when he wants, then I'm not sure he would have been prepared to wait,' said Ginger.

'Hmm, perhaps. We can put him in the maybe column.'

'Okay, who's next? Matt?' Ginger looked concerned as she spoke. 'After we met him, I wasn't so convinced about his guilt, but he's had a troubled relationship with Kenneth based on money and drugs. That's not a good combination and both can cause people to react in extreme ways. We know Nancy hasn't spoken to the police about Matt's disagreement with Kenneth and I doubt she ever will. If the police are still of the opinion that Kenneth is the victim of a burglary gone wrong, then I don't know how else they would find out those details. I don't feel good about any of that. Part of me feels sorry for Matt, part of me wants to point at him and declare that *he did it.*' Whatever happened, Ginger felt Matt needed more help than he was getting, and perhaps a firm hand to steer him. Although Tobias seemed to be trying that.

'We can't forget he tried to run us over,' Joyce reminded her.

'He claims that wasn't him.'

'He would say that, wouldn't he?'

'And anyway, last night you said you genuinely believed him when he said he *hadn't* tried to run us over.'

Joyce gave a grunt of acknowledgement. 'Okay, that leaves Nancy and Robert.'

Ginger thought for a minute before replying. 'I would have said that the idea of Nancy harming Kenneth was ridiculous, but I don't understand why she hasn't told us that she was around back in the '50s and knew everyone.'

'I wouldn't go that far. She appeared in a couple of photographs, in the background. It might just be coincidence.'

'I doubt it.' Ginger was finding all this a bit much. Half a cup of coffee just wasn't enough. If she was at home, she might have crawled back into bed with a newspaper, a couple of slices of toast and a pot of coffee on the bedside table so she didn't have to get up when she wanted a top-up. Instead, she was being forced to identify a killer. She was as curious as Joyce; she just needed another hour for the caffeine to hit her eyeballs, and then she could resemble a fully functioning human being.

'Let's just ask her,' declared Joyce with a burst of energy that unsettled Ginger.

'Do we have to? I don't want to traipse all the way across London, again.'

'What do you think telephones are for, Ginger dear? They're all the rage now, you know, and you don't even need a piece of string connecting them in order for them to work.' Joyce pulled her mobile phone out of her pocket while Ginger willed the caffeine to work.

39

'*I* hope this isn't too early,' said Joyce after Nancy had picked up the phone. She wasn't really bothered if it was, and anyway, it was 8.30 in the morning so it wasn't that bad.

'Not at all, I was just finishing my cup of tea before I go and do some shopping. I've spent so much time thinking about Kenneth that I forgot to go shopping and the fridge is bare. I really must do something about that, especially if Matt drops round. He has such an enormous appetite.' She went suddenly quiet for a moment. 'Is that why you're calling me, to talk about Matt and my silly ideas?'

'No, no, not that. There's something else we want to talk to you about.'

'We?' Nancy sounded confused.

'Ginger is here with me.'

'Morning, Nancy,' Ginger called in confirmation.

'Oh hello, Ginger, good morning.'

'Nancy, I wanted to ask, how did you meet Kenneth?'

'Oh well, that was a long time ago. A friend of mine knew him, I can't remember how. Anyway, he was looking for someone to clean and take on a few extra jobs. I hadn't worked for a while and was rather nervous, but she told me what a lovely man he was and that it would be okay. She was right, he was very charming and patient with me. Mind you, the cleaning part wasn't a problem. It sounds strange to a lot of people, but I love cleaning. I like that sense of achievement when you can look around a room and it's sparkling.'

After allowing the silence that followed to stretch, Joyce simply said, 'No, Nancy. I meant the *first* time you met.'

'What?' Now the woman on the other end of the phone sounded really confused.

'We know you met him, and my mother, at the theatre.'

The silence continued after Joyce had spoken, eventually broken by a sigh from Nancy.

'I didn't tell you about meeting your mother because, well, it wasn't the nicest of circumstances and I didn't think you needed to know, that she would want you to know. You see…'

'I know what happened, you don't need to explain. You prevented an attack on my mother, thank you.' More than anything, Joyce didn't want Nancy to have to go through the possibly agonising experience of what had happened while talking to the daughter of the woman concerned. 'Go on, Nancy.'

'I only met Kenneth very briefly; he didn't actually remember our meeting when I told him about it while we met to discuss the job. That's how brief it was.'

Joyce and Ginger exchanged glances. But then, Audrey hadn't seemed too certain when she'd said it had been Kenneth whom Nancy had known backstage. A silent communication passed between the two women. They were inclined to believe Nancy.

'My best friend was a Tiller Girl and sometimes invited me backstage, and she did so that night,' Nancy was saying. 'But the place was like a rabbit warren and I got lost on the way to the bathroom and went into the wrong room – that's how I came across your mother and Scroop. I met Kenneth to say hello to that night, but that was all, and then I went dancing with a group of friends.

'I know that Scroop was killed that night, but it was much more memorable to me for personal reasons. You see, I met my Reg and we were married two years later. My friend met her fella through the theatre too. Well, our son went on to marry their daughter, so me and my best friend were both grandmother to Matt. But Daff – my friend – she died a couple of years ago. I do miss her, but her fella is still around and, of course, I see him at the occasional family get-together.'

There was a warmth in her voice as she spoke of family and friends. Joyce looked over at Ginger, who gave a nod. It seemed that they were in agreement. Nancy was definitely telling them the truth.

'Why didn't you mention any of this before?' asked Ginger, with clear curiosity and no frustration in her voice.

'I thought it would complicate things, you see. Like I said, I met Kenneth so briefly that he couldn't remember it. Daff and I went off to a party almost straight away – once I knew your mum was back with her friends, Joyce, and Scroop couldn't get near her. So I didn't know anything about the murder of Scroop.'

Joyce couldn't argue with her. Nancy's revelations might have saved her and Ginger from some last-minute concerns, but they didn't actually add anything to their knowledge. They certainly didn't tell them who had killed Scroop, or Kenneth for that matter; they were just the tendrils of friendships and families that had got entwined a long time ago with no real effect on the present.

Joyce felt a little flat. She had rather hoped that Nancy would have important information which could send them on the final leg of their investigation or set off a revelatory spark so they'd know immediately who had done it. But they weren't any further along.

40

*T*he day had dragged for Ginger. Frustrated by their lack of success, she was distracted as she went for a stroll along the Thames. After a quick visit to the Turner exhibition, she hopped onto a Tube and made her way to the Victoria and Albert Museum to look at the costume and fashion exhibitions, but they didn't grab her attention as they ordinarily would.

Joyce had gone on her final shopping trip. Although Ginger had enjoyed a quiet lunch on her own at an Italian restaurant, with a glass of white wine and a rather large serving of Tiramisu for dessert, she remained preoccupied and unable to think of anything other than Kenneth's murder. Joyce had remained as vocal and upbeat about her planned purchases as ever, but Ginger could spot an edge to her mood too. They hadn't known each other all that long, they didn't have decades of friendship behind them, but Ginger knew her friend well enough to see that Joyce was concerned.

It made sense that Joyce was keen to see this mystery resolved. She wanted to lay the ghosts of the past to rest and work out who had killed her mother's friend. This was personal for Joyce. Ginger had half expected Joyce to declare that she would remain in London until the case had been solved, but she had yet to make that statement.

There were a good few hours to go yet before they departed for home the next day and there was bound to be more alcohol involved this evening. Who knew what course of action Joyce might decide upon when the emotions and alcohol collided? Not that Ginger was worried; she would welcome a sense of purpose, some movement and a few possibly ill-judged decisions made under the influence of Joyce's favourite sparkling wine, which might just give them the final burst of energy they needed. Once lubricated, the brain cells could come up with a few left-field ideas and reveal the final clue.

These thoughts gave her a little hope. As she returned to the flat to dress for dinner, she had a more discernible spring in her step.

Their final dinner in the city was at another French brasserie-style restaurant, surrounded by Art Deco and with a killer cock-tail list, and Ginger had been dying to go there for ages. They'd remembered to reserve a table and, after placing their orders, they sighed in unison then smiled at one another.

'We can still give this our time when we are back in Derbyshire,' said Ginger, trying to sound reassuring. 'We're not walking away from it, not entirely.'

Joyce shrugged. 'Oh, I know. I just don't like leaving things unfinished.'

'Or not getting things your own way.' Ginger gave a little lopsided smile and hoped Joyce would see the funny side.

'Yes alright, that too. We have everything we need, I know we do. We could use one of those big displays of photographs and maps with string connecting things; we could stare at it and the answer would suddenly leap out at us.'

Ginger was now imagining them as American detectives in a smoky basement room, Joyce looking mean with a cigarette hanging out of her mouth. It was not a difficult image to conjure up.

'It's the scooter; that will tie it all together for us. Matt said it wasn't him and I believe him, reluctantly. The boy still has an attitude that doesn't impress me. So, either we mistook the scooter and it was never his in the first place, or someone else was riding it.'

'We should have asked him if he ever lends it to anyone.'

Joyce put her hands in the air in a display of exasperation. 'I know, we're idiots. We can always speak to him again.'

The server arrived at the table with their cocktails.

'One Airmail,' he said as he placed the glass in front of Joyce, 'and a Chrysanthemum.'

Ginger smiled up at him. 'Thank you.' They clinked their glasses and each took a long sip.

'That looks like a urine sample,' said Joyce, looking at the pale-yellow liquid Ginger was drinking.

'Thanks for that, it's actually very tasty.'

'What on earth is in it?'

'Dry vermouth, Benedictine and absinthe.'

'Isn't that what Van Gogh was drinking when he cut his ear off?'

Ginger shook her head. 'That's a myth, so you don't have to worry about me grabbing your steak knife and bleeding all over dinner.'

Joyce returned to looking distracted for a few minutes before coming to a decision.

'Once we've had dinner, shall we go and say goodbye to Jim? We're only ten minutes' walk away from the Palladium.'

'And pick his brains one more time?'

'That too. Now then, what am I drinking next? This is our last night, we should make the most of it.'

Ginger took a deep breath. She'd be sure to have plenty to eat or it could be a messy last night in the city.

41

*O*nce they had finished dinner, had an espresso each in an attempt to balance out the alcohol, and argued over the dessert they were going to share, which was simply resolved by dropping the charade that they were trying to be sensible and ordering one each (a Black Forest gateau which Ginger would remember for years to come and a mountain of profiteroles for Joyce), they set off to the London Palladium theatre. Joyce didn't lead them straight to the stage door; she wanted to stand outside the main entrance for a moment, gazing at the classical temple front with its Corinthian columns. The gold detailing against the white stone; the sculpture at the top of the pediment; the row of lights above the entrance.

Tonight, the theatre was 'dark'; there were no performances as it prepared for a big show opening next week, so there wasn't the usual feeling of something magical taking place inside. But the building itself remained magical for Joyce. She tried to imagine what it was like to be here in the '40s and '50s when her mother was performing: the crowds bustling outside, dressed in the style of the time, excited to see the dancers; her mother backstage getting ready. Ginger said nothing, giving her the time she needed, and she appreciated her friend's patience.

As they walked round the side of the building, Ginger pointed over the road. On the far side of the street was a motorcycle parking bay, and in the middle of a row of motorbikes of all shapes and sizes was a navy-blue scooter with a white mudguard. A couple of yards away was a large Irish pub, part of a chain that Joyce would never normally venture into.

'Chances are Matt's in there. We should go and find him after this, ask him a couple more questions.'

Ginger just nodded.

Jim's little cubbyhole office was empty when they arrived.

'He'll be back in a minute,' said a young man who was rolling a cigarette. 'Can I help?'

'No, thank you. We're friends of Jim, we'll just wait.' Joyce positioned herself next to the counter and, out of curiosity, scanned down the list of names in the visitors' sign-in book. There was no one she recognised and nothing of interest. More retirement cards had gone on display since their last visit and a bouquet of flowers sat on top of a filing cabinet. Jim must have a matter of weeks, if not days left until he retired.

Joyce considered how much of his life the theatre had filled. It wasn't just a job; it must be a home and a family too. She scanned the photos on the walls and tried to imagine what the office would be like once Jim took them all home. It would be a cold little corner without the weight of his personality and history. Many of the photos featured Jim, and she could follow his life through them as he appeared at different ages, standing next to musicians, actors and singers, from The Beatles and Cliff Richard to the cast of *Cats*.

There was a photo of Jim with a young boy sitting on his lap, Joyce assumed his son or grandson. Probably grandson based on how old Jim looked. A woman, most likely his wife, beamed out of a picture on his desk; the same woman sat behind him in a photo of him astride an old motorbike. In all of them, Jim looked cheerful; he appeared to be relishing every opportunity life threw at him. Joyce rather envied him his obvious simple enthusiasm for everything he encountered.

She wondered what her mother had made of the naïve young lad who ran around backstage, letting the performers know how long they had until they were due on stage and being teased by all the dancers. Joyce imagined that her mother would have been charmed by Jim, but kept an eye out in case the teasing got a little cruel. Then she would have stepped in.

'Ladies, ladies, ladies, what a bonus.' The warm voice echoed down the corridor. Jim was smartly dressed as always in dark trousers, a shirt and tie, which had London buses all over it. Joyce smiled at it, despite its inherent tackiness.

'We came to say goodbye, we leave tomorrow.'

There was a pause before Jim replied. 'Oh well, I am sorry to hear that. It would have been nice to get to know Margaret's lovely daughter better, but it's been magical to get any time at all with you. I'm chuffed that you came to introduce yourself to me. It brought back a lot of memories. I'm just sorry that your trip might have been dampened by what happened to poor Kenneth. It was all very sad.'

He stepped back to allow a man carrying a pile of boxes past him.

'Talking of Kenneth, is there anything you can remember from way back?' asked Joyce. 'Anyone who might have had a grudge against him and would still be alive now?'

Jim looked at her intently, as though he was trying to read her mind.

'Looking for answers, to help people, just like your mother.' He sighed and shook his head. 'No, he was a nice man. Polite, treated people well. If you're looking for a connection between

Scroop's death and Kenneth's, then I can't imagine what it could be; the two men couldn't have been more different. Kenneth must have just got in someone's way, his death very unfortunate and regrettable. Unlike Scroop who deserved all he got.'

Joyce suddenly felt very tired. She wasn't going to get any further. She looked over at Ginger, who was gazing curiously around Jim's office.

'Ginger? Shall we make a move?'

'Hmm, sure.' Ginger paused before appearing to have an idea. 'Let's get a photo of you both, over here. It'll be nice to have all the cards and flowers in the background.' She put her hand out to Joyce, who gave her her mobile phone.

Jim beamed. 'Oh yes, wonderful, and you must be sure to send me a copy,' he said. 'I'll add it to the collection when I take it all home. It will go next to the photograph of me and your mother, Joyce.'

Ginger positioned them, moving them a few inches one way, then an inch or two the other. When she was happy, she took a few photos and smiled.

'You both look lovely.'

'Don't forget to send me a copy, Ginger.'

'Don't worry, I'll make sure you get one.'

There was a slight edge to Ginger's voice as she replied to Jim, which took Joyce by surprise. They both said goodbye to him and promised to get in touch when they were next in the city. As they stepped out onto the street, Ginger grabbed Joyce's arm and started to tug her away from the stage door.

'What on earth…'

'We need to talk, away from here…'

'HELP, I'm being kidnapped.' Joyce hadn't shouted too loudly, but she still turned the heads of passers-by. Ginger pulled her to a table outside the Irish pub and within sight of the scooter they had seen parked earlier.

'Give me back your phone,' she demanded.

'Why? What are…'

'Now!' Ginger was sounding increasingly desperate. Taken by surprise, Joyce did as she was asked without any more argument and Ginger pulled something up on the phone. She handed it to Joyce, who found herself staring at the photo of her and Jim. It was a nice photograph and Ginger was right: the background of cards and flowers gave it a celebratory edge. If she zoomed in, she could make out the photograph of her mother. Everything about it was perfect and she was unsure what Ginger was so flustered about.

Then she saw it. She paused, sitting down at the pub table, trying to understand why it was important, why a part of her brain was now spinning. It was just a motorcycle helmet on a shelf. Why was that…

'Oh hell.' Joyce looked up at Ginger, knowing what she had been getting at.

42

*A*fter the two women had gone back and forth over what they had come to realise and gradually pieced everything together, they both had one question.

'What do we do now?' they asked in chorus.

'Hello!' They looked up at Matt, who had approached their table. 'Alright?'

'Very well, thank you,' replied Joyce. 'Have you ridden here?' She glanced at the scooter and the helmet in his hand.

'No, I'm picking it up from Grandad.'

'Your grandad rides?'

'Yeah, he got it for me, but borrows it sometimes.'

Ginger thought hard, running over the course of events from the last few days and trying to identify a date.

'Did he borrow it on Thursday?'

Matt looked confused for a moment. 'Er, yeah, yeah he did.'

'And where did you meet him to pick it up?'

Another pause as Matt thought. 'We went to a pub. It was pretty late, but we were in time for last orders. I wouldn't have bothered, but I needed it the next day.'

'That pub doesn't happen to be up near the Strand, does it?' Ginger already knew the answer.

'Yeah, yeah, it is, the Rose and Crown. They do a decent pint, and like Grandad says, it's nice riding at that time of night. Quiet, less traffic around.'

No traffic, just a couple of old birds to run over, Ginger thought. By now the three of them had walked away from the pub table and were standing next to the scooter, and Ginger felt herself shiver. She'd largely blocked out the events of that night and how she'd been lucky not to end up with anything worse than a slight strain, but it came back to her now.

She pushed the thoughts away again. Ginger knew the answer to her next question as well, but she needed to ask it all the same.

'Who is your grandfather, Matt?'

Before he could answer, there was a shout from over the road.

'Matt! Alright there, lad?' Jim Nevin waved a set of keys in the air, a big grin on his face. He spotted Joyce and Ginger and gave them a grin too, but it wasn't returned. They stared back sternly, which clearly gave him cause to hesitate. Then he spun around and headed back to the door he'd appeared from.

Ginger didn't wait and took off after him. He was older than her and she was fitter than she looked; he didn't stand a chance. She dashed across the road followed by Joyce, who was remarkably quick on a pair of stilettos, but then she wore nothing else, so was well practised. Matt was behind them, shouting for answers.

Ginger followed Jim through the stage door entrance and was close enough to see him disappear through a second door beyond his desk. She managed to grab it before it clicked shut and they were thwarted by a key pad. Holding it open with her foot for Joyce, she ran in the direction she'd seen Jim head off in once she knew that Joyce was safely through.

They were now in the kind of environment Ginger was familiar with: dark narrow corridors, walls painted black. When the spaces opened out, there were usually two white lines that formed a path, ensuring that no one could dump anything and block the route, which could be lethal in the dark when a show was on. Ginger wondered momentarily if Jim was going to lead them to the stage, but that was unlikely; it would be full of technicians getting ready for the next production.

They turned corners and ran through a number of doors. The backstage of theatres could accurately be compared with a rabbit warren, but the comforting familiarity of the environment made it less confusing or frightening for Ginger. She could still hear Joyce's heels on the floor behind her, along with the words that were turning the air blue, and hoped she could get to Jim before her friend.

Jim was surprisingly agile for his age, but he was slowing as he set off down a staircase. He had the advantage of knowing this place like the back of his hand. Ginger wasn't afraid; she didn't think for one minute that there was any risk of him doing anything stupid, but she did want answers.

'Jim, stop,' she called as she ran down the stairs. 'This is ridiculous.' The sound of Joyce clomping down behind her, continuing to call Jim every name under the sun, was making Ginger want to laugh; the whole thing was ludicrous. Three old codgers running pointlessly around the backstage area of a theatre with a young bloke in motorcycle kit trailing after them. All they needed was a bit of comedy music in the background and the picture would be complete.

'Jim, for heaven's sake…' Ginger burst through a set of doors into a dark room, and nearly ran face first into a rack of metal shelves. 'Bleedin' hell.' Joyce ran into the back of her and they fumbled around, keeping one another upright.

'Hang on, I'll find the light switch.' Ginger disentangled herself from Joyce's waving arms and felt around the wall, quickly finding a switch and bathing the low-ceilinged room in a dim yellow glow. It was a small room with shelves all around it, which appeared to be for storing lighting equipment. Lights of all shapes and sizes, cables and boxes of unidentifiable electrical equipment lined the walls, and on the far side, out of breath, was Jim.

All four of them stood for a moment or two, catching their breath. The running had finally caught up with them.

'Are you all crazy?' exclaimed Matt.

'They are,' replied Joyce, waving a finger at the other two. 'Don't you dare go putting me in the same category as them.'

Matt looked utterly confused. 'Grandad, what's going on? Why were you running? What the hell…?'

Ginger spotted a chair in the corner. It was covered in dust, but she wiped it with her hand and sat down.

'That's better. Now, I agree with your grandson's question: what's going on, Jim? Why did you try and mow us down with the scooter?' Ginger knew, and she knew Joyce knew too. They'd finally worked it out, but Jim had to say it out loud; they didn't have much in the way of solid evidence, so needed Jim to confess.

'I did no such thing.'

'Alright, why did you try to give us a scare by *pretending* to mow us down?'

'Is that why you borrowed my scooter?'

Jim looked at his grandson, but didn't answer. Joyce stepped forward and looked around the room; Ginger guessed she was looking for a chair, but there wasn't another one, and Ginger wasn't giving hers up.

Joyce sighed. 'Alright, Jim, I'll tell you what we think happened and you can just confirm or deny it.' From the way Jim looked at Joyce, he seemed to be taking her instructions seriously. Ginger was sure that Joyce being the daughter of Margaret Brocklehurst, and looking very much like her, made him behave differently.

'It's very simple, really: Kenneth had taken over Sheridan's pet project of trying to work out who had killed Scroop Harrison de

Clare. No one would blame the person who killed him; it wasn't about tracking down a killer and bringing him, or her, to justice, but Sheridan was curious. He was an old man with time on his hands, probably living in his memories of the past, and he really wanted to know who it was. When he died, Kenneth took over, but unlike Sheridan, he worked it out. He realised that you killed Scroop.'

'What's she talking about?'

'Sorry, Matt, it would have been better if you weren't here for this.'

The young man glared at Joyce. 'This is rubbish.'

'If it's rubbish, we owe your grandfather a huge apology, and then we'll be on our way and the whole thing can be forgotten. But think about this: why did he run when he saw us talking to you, and how is it that someone on your distinctive scooter tried to run us over on the evening that you loaned it to your grandfather?'

She didn't wait for an answer and turned back to Jim. 'Jim, your job in the '50s meant you went everywhere at the theatre and no one ever questioned your presence. You were meant to be running all over the place, and anyway, you were a young lad. No one was going to even think of you as a possible suspect. You were practically invisible.

'You must have seen and heard all sorts of things back then, been privy to everyone's secrets, and as a sixteen-year-old lad, you probably didn't care all that much, except when it affected your beloved Tiller Girls. Especially my mother. You probably saw more of Scroop's bad behaviour than anyone: the way he treated women and people like Kenneth. It must have made you so angry, then one night, you witnessed him threatening Kenneth and that made you really mad.

'It wasn't long after that that a very young Nancy turned up to see her friend, Daff, perform. They were closer to your age, and you and Daff – or rather, *Daphne* – had caught one another's eye.

I didn't twig at first when Nancy told me about her best friend, and the husband she met through the theatre, and the grandson they shared, but of course! Daff, short for Daphne, and you yourself referred to your beloved Daphne who passed a couple of years ago.

'So, did Nancy tell you what she had seen when she disturbed Margaret and Scroop, or did it get to you via Daphne? It doesn't matter, but you found out that Scroop had tried to attack my mother, the woman you idolised. The woman you yourself and everyone else says you would have done anything for. You were enraged and it was uncontrollable.

'You could have made up any number of excuses to get Scroop alone. After all, you delivered messages all the time, so you telling him that someone wanted to see him, to follow you, that was nothing unusual. In the dark corridors, you knew your way and you could take him into the depths of the theatre, kill him, and hide his body. This wasn't murder to you; you were protecting the people who you viewed as family. People you loved, and in your own way, you loved my mother.'

Matt strode over to Jim and stood by him.

'This is ridiculous, all of it. You have no evidence.'

Jim glanced at him, gave him a brief pat on the shoulder, and then turned back to Joyce.

'He was an evil man. You're right, I'd witnessed things the others didn't know anything about. They knew about the way he treated Audrey, but they didn't actually see her getting a black eye. I did. I saw him harass countless young women. I saw him treat men he viewed as beneath him with contempt. I was invisible to him; after all, I was just a kid. And you're right when you say I could go anywhere I wanted and people rarely noticed.

'Scroop had it coming to him. I don't regret what I did, I'd do it again. I was convinced that the police would work it out. Everyone thought I was just in shock because I'd never known anyone who was killed before, but it wasn't that. I was in shock at what I'd done; I was terrified that I was going to get caught. But after the weeks had passed and the police hadn't come for me, things started to get back to normal. Hardly anyone talked about him, no one missed him. I just got on with my life. I always knew I'd done the right thing.'

'And Kenneth?' asked Joyce.

There was silence as Jim looked at the floor, then at Matt, and finally back at Joyce.

'Kenneth? I am sorry about that.'

43

*J*oyce couldn't feel angry at Jim for killing Scroop. She knew she should; it was a life taken, after all. Scroop should have been stopped by confrontation, not murder. But still, she wasn't entirely sure that she wouldn't have done the same thing given the opportunity, so who was she to judge? But Kenneth, that was a different matter. She wanted to grab hold of Jim and…

She forced herself to take a deep breath, all the while staring at him. He looked old and tired and leaned back against some shelving. A lamp on the shelf above him shifted slightly and Joyce wondered if it would fall and hit him; she didn't care. Just like earlier in Jim's office when, she suspected now, she'd known the truth deep down inside, Joyce suddenly felt very tired herself.

'Why kill Kenneth?' she asked. Before Jim could answer, a man in a baseball cap walked into the room. He came to a sudden stop and took in the scene before him. Joyce glared at him so ferociously that he left without anyone saying a word.

She turned back to Jim.

'I didn't want to, it wasn't the plan. I went round to see him; he'd been asking a lot of questions about Scroop, calling people, and he came to see me a couple of times. We were having a right laugh like only old friends can, but I must have said something. I don't know what it was, but it was like a light went on. He realised it was me that killed Scroop. He asked me outright; I denied it, but he kept pushing.'

Jim looked at Matt and as he did so, it was as though he shrank in size. His shoulders dropped and the avenging angel who had been so sure he'd done the right thing in killing Scroop seemed to turn into a guilty man who knew he deserved to be punished; who was too tired to run; who had given up. Joyce watched as Ginger stood up and took the chair over to him. Jim gave a weak smile of thanks and sat down.

'I didn't want to give up this.' Jim put his hands in the air and looked up the ceiling. 'The theatre has been my entire life. I was a kid when I started and now I'm eighty-five. I've loved every minute of it. Everyone knows me; everyone looks forward to seeing me when they come back to work here. I make them feel at home. I'm a friendly face, a familiar face. I'm godfather to nineteen kids, all of their parents people I've met working at the stage door. I'm part of their family. When Daphne passed... well, it's only working here that kept me going. Okay, I know I am about to retire, but I would still have the love of my family, my friends. I would still have my memories, my reputation. If Kenneth had told people what I'd done, I would have lost all that. I couldn't have that. Scroop, I don't regret, but Kenneth... I'm sorry, I had no choice.'

Joyce felt a cold chill creep across her body. She hated Jim for what he had done to Kenneth, but before her was a tired old man. A tiny part of her felt sorry for him. Running around trying to solve a murder had a touch of Agatha Christie about it, until she found herself face to face with the grim reality. Nothing about it was fun or even slightly interesting now.

Matt walked across the room towards the door. Joyce grabbed his shoulder as he passed her.

'Where are you going?'

'What business is that of yours?'

'He needs you.'

'He can sod off, I don't want anything else to do with him.' Matt shoved the door open and they could hear him running up the stairs. Joyce hoped he'd come round; he didn't need to forgive his grandfather, but he could at least bring himself to remain in Jim's life.

Ginger picked Joyce's bag up off the floor and dug out the mobile phone.

'Will you be alright on your own?' she asked as she took hold of the door handle.

Joyce nodded. 'The detective's card is in my purse.'

'Always optimistic.' Ginger smiled, and then retrieved it and left to find a stronger phone signal at ground level.

Joyce had nothing left to say to Jim, but she moved closer to him. They remained in silence, Joyce wishing she knew what her mother would have said to the man who had once been her most ardent young admirer.

44

*E*very woman in the line smiled broadly, their arms around one another as they kicked in perfect unison, all turning with the one in the middle forming the central pivot. The black-and-white film hid the colours of their costumes, but it couldn't hide the shimmer of the sequins and the glow that shone from each of them.

'Your mother missed appearing on TV by one year,' Audrey told them. 'This is the one performance I gave that was filmed before I hung up my dancing shoes. Your mother said she didn't mind, but I'm rather pleased that I have this record. The grand-children used to make me play it over and over again when they were little.'

Audrey's eyes didn't leave the screen as she spoke. 'I remember when we first started, we couldn't afford stockings so we used to put wet white on our legs. Awfully messy stuff, it was methylated spirits, glycerine, zinc oxide and rosewater. It was freezing cold when you first put it on. All our legs had to be the same colour, you see.'

'You must have been very fit,' said Ginger. She was exhausted just watching them.

'Oh, we were. I look back in awe of my younger self.'

Ginger wondered if Joyce was sorry her mother wasn't there on the screen, but she seemed to be alright.

'Did you not want to follow in your mother's footsteps, or should I say dance steps?' asked Audrey. Joyce shook her head.

'No, I did dance as a child, but once I started to notice boys, well, that put paid to that.' Audrey smiled with a look of understanding. 'Also, I can't bear to take orders. Taking them from my mother was one thing, but I wouldn't listen to anybody else.'

'You still won't,' Ginger chipped in.

'Too flippin' right,' Joyce confirmed.

They watched a few more minutes of the film in silence, Ginger starting to wonder if perhaps it was time she went to a few yoga lessons, or perhaps a dance class. She didn't only groan when she pulled herself out of a chair these days, but as she sat down too. She was also still feeling the after-effects of dancing at the milonga. If she did something like that more often, perhaps she'd be a bit more flexible. She promised herself she would give it some serious thought once she got back home.

'Were the police very annoyed at you?' Audrey's question took Ginger by surprise.

'Annoyed?'

'Yes, well, you beat them to it. Rather embarrassed them, I imagine.'

Ginger smiled as she recalled the expressions on the two detectives' faces. She wasn't sure, but she had thought she'd seen a little smile on the sergeant's; he'd looked ever so slightly impressed. Detective Grumpy had remained the miserable, silent type.

'I do remember Jim, or little Jimmy as we called him. He couldn't do enough to help us; he was rather in awe of us all, I think. He mustn't have been able to believe his luck when one of the dancers agreed to go out with him. Daphne was a lovely girl, two years younger than me. We were all very pleased for him, and it was quite a relief. He was so enamoured by the dancers – especially your mother, of course, Joyce – that we were afraid he wouldn't be able to move beyond the fantasy, but Daphne was very sweet and they seemed perfectly suited. To think she died not having a clue that Jim had killed Scroop. Well, I assume she didn't.'

'I doubt it. I don't think that Jim had told a soul until he confessed everything to us. It actually felt like it was a bit of a relief for him.'

Ginger nodded; she agreed with Joyce. Jim had been so worried about anyone finding out that he'd killed Scroop, but it must have been a dreadful burden to carry with him throughout his life all the same.

'It doesn't surprise me, you know, Joyce.'

'What's that, Audrey?'

'That you – and you too, Ginger – worked it out. Your mother was a very bright, very determined woman. We all admired her, and it didn't surprise a single one of us that she carved her own path in life, despite making choices that in those days were frowned upon and that there was very little support for, moral or practical. She loved you and your sister and she was determined to give you a good life, and lead the life she wanted. She certainly did that and I can see exactly the same determination in you. And you, Ginger. She'd have been very proud of you.'

Joyce smiled and sat back in her chair, her eyes fixed on the dancers on the screen.

After lunch with Audrey, Joyce and Ginger made their way to Euston Station. They were booked on an afternoon train back to Manchester, where they would get a local connection into Derbyshire.

'At least this train isn't too early,' said Joyce as she plonked a bottle of champagne on the table. 'Do you think we'll be able to get a couple of glasses? This is first class, after all.' She leaned out into the aisle. 'I don't want to have to go and fetch them, but if someone doesn't hurry up, I'm just going to drink it straight from the bottle.'

Ginger was rooting around in her bag. 'Did I ever tell you I used to be a Girl Guide?'

'Many times, but what has that got to do with the price of milk?'

'Always prepared, and I've spent enough time with you to know what that looks like.' Ginger pulled two robust plastic champagne flutes from her bag. The base of the stem was detachable and she swiftly put the pieces together.

'*Et voilà*! Impressed or what?'

'Plastic? Plastic?'

'Stop whingeing, for heaven's sake. It's that or you neck it straight from the bottle and I know you have standards. Not many, but one or two.'

Halfway through the journey and the bottle was empty. The two women were drawing up a list of places they wanted to go together. New York, Sydney and Barcelona had all been easy to agree upon. Joyce was typically vocal about the fact she wasn't as keen on Ginger's desire to climb Machu Picchu, and Ginger was refusing to go to Paris during fashion week. She wanted to go, yes, but not when the city was overrun with women who ate a grain of rice for dinner and everyone wore clothing that looked as if the designer had been high on drugs when they'd come up with the idea.

'How about Buenos Aires?' Ginger suggested. 'We could go dancing. I rather enjoyed the milonga; I fancy a bit more of that, and how perfect would it be to dance the night away on a hot and steamy floor in Argentina?'

Joyce didn't look entirely put off by the idea. 'So long as you don't expect me to dance with you again.'

'What are you complaining about? We had a blast and we

made a good couple. Come on.' She reached for Joyce's phone and tried to unlock it; she knew the code, she'd seen it often enough, but on top of all the wine they'd had at lunch, the champagne was a bit too much and Ginger wasn't having much luck hitting the right numbers.

'Give it to me.' Joyce unlocked it and handed it back. 'What are you trying to do?'

'Music maestro,' Ginger declared. She didn't own a phone as fancy as Joyce's, but she had been put in charge of the music in a number of theatre rehearsals, which meant operating someone else's all-singing, all-dancing technology. She searched for a moment, and then found what she was looking for. Turning the volume up, she hit play. The carriage was filled with the sounds of the Argentinian tango.

'Ginger Salt, turn that down.'

'Not a chance.' Ginger stuck the phone in her pocket, then stood up. The other passengers looked a mix of fascinated and annoyed. 'Come on, dance. You're dressed for it.'

Joyce's travel outfit was a scarlet red trouser suit, its close fit bound to get a few hearts racing.

'Don't be so blooming ridiculous, Ginger. Now sit down before you get us thrown off the train.'

'Not much chance of that.' Ginger nodded down the aisle at the train conductor leaning against the door with a grin on his face. He'd made a number of excuses to stop and chat to them each time he went past, focusing his attention almost entirely on Joyce.

'It's a ridiculous idea and there isn't any room, so it's impossible.'

'This is first class, so there are a few extra inches of room and we can improvise... I know you want to, my dear Joyce Brocklehurst, and you really should, otherwise I might tell a few of your colleagues at that beautiful stately home about an incident with a dress and a security tag.'

'And I'll tell them you made it all up.'

'And I'll show them photos.'

'You don't have… what do you mean? You don't, do you?' Joyce's eyes were on stalks and Ginger grinned a lopsided champagne grin. She watched the painful – or funny, depending on your point of view – reality dawn on Joyce's face. With an expression like thunder, Joyce got out of her seat, pulled her jacket straight, threw her shoulders back and, with faultless style, grabbed Ginger and cha-cha-chaaed her down the aisle of the first-class carriage on the 15.32 from London Euston.

If you enjoyed *Murder in the Wings* sign up to Kate P Adams' newsletter at www.katepadams.com to find out when the next in the series is available to buy, and get a free mystery.

HAVE YOU READ THE CHARLETON HOUSE MYSTERIES?

Read the books that first featured Joyce Brocklehurst

Death by Dark Roast.

The annual Charleton House Food Festival is about to begin. But the first item on the menu is murder...

Nestled in the idyllic setting of Derbyshire's rolling hills, the ancestral home of the Fitzwilliam-Scott family seems an unlikely location for murder. But when a young man is bludgeoned to death with the portafilter of a coffee machine, recent thefts from local stately homes are put in the shade, and caffeine-loving café manager Sophie Lockwood finds her interest piqued by a pair of unusual cases.

Readers say:

'I absolutely adored this book!'

'The mysteries are fascinating and the writing is as elegant as Charleton House itself. A brilliant series I will read every word of.'

READ A FREE CHARLETON HOUSE MYSTERY

Building a relationship with my readers is one of the best things about writing. I occasionally send newsletters with details on new releases, special offers, interviews and articles relating to my books.

Sign up to my mailing list and you'll also receive the very first Charleton House Mystery, *A Stately Murder*.

Head to my website for your free copy and find out what happens when Sophie stumbles across the victim of the first murder Charleton House has ever known.

www.katepadams.com

ABOUT THE AUTHOR

After 25 years working in some of England's finest buildings, Kate P. Adams has turned to murder.

Kate grew up in Derbyshire, the setting for many of her books, and went on to work in theatres around the country, the Natural History Museum - London, the University of Oxford and Hampton Court Palace. Every day she explored darkened corridors and rooms full of history behind doors the public never get to enter. Kate spent years in these beautiful buildings listening to fantastic tales, wondering where the bodies were hidden, and hoping that she'd run into a ghost or two.

Kate has an unhealthy obsession with finding the perfect cup of coffee, enjoys a gin and tonic, and is managed by Pumpkin, a domineering tabby cat who is a little on the large side. Now that she lives in the USA, writing allows Kate to go home to her beloved Derbyshire every day, in her head at least.

www.katepadams.com

Printed in Great Britain
by Amazon

11096347R00125